I0671923

WEIRD HORROR MAGAZINE

AUTUMN 2024

ISSUE 9

Edited by

MICHAEL KELLY

UNDERTOW
PUBLICATIONS

WEIRD HORROR 9
Autumn 2024

PUBLISHER
Undertow Publications

EDITOR/LAYOUT
Michael Kelly

PROOFREADER
Carolyn Macdonell

OPINION
Simon Strantzas

COMMENTARY
Orrin Grey

BOOKS
Lysette Stevenson

ART
David Nickle

COVER DESIGN
Vince Haig

Weirdhorrormagazine.com

Contents

On Horror

Simon Strantzas

The Fantastique and the Weird

I BELIEVE Clive Barker's writing was an inflection point for horror fiction. I also suspect Clive Barker was mostly disinterested in Horror and took advantage of opportunities afforded because the genre had an inflated popularity at the end of the twentieth century, and there was a chance to make easy money and/or to bootstrap a burgeoning career.

I don't necessarily see this as a problem, though. After all, he irrevocably changed the genre. Barker introduced a perversity into Horror, especially North American Horror, bringing in the S&M-leather/neon-sex-club vibe that had already influenced music and film. Much of it, of course, was the media co-opting gay culture — similar to how it had co-opted Black culture — but because Horror fiction in America was and remains predominately conservative, one would have expected it to be immune to such outsider influences. However, Barker's work was too imaginative and versatile and discomforting to ignore, and the door he cracked open allowed subsequent horror stories to explore less conservative ideas.

And I'd also argue that it was specifically his apparent disinterest in the genre that made Barker so revolutionary. While he struck his mark with the BOOKS OF BLOOD — a series of short horror stories that explored the breadth of the genre, from quiet to extreme — he quickly moved away from writing something so easily categorized. Famously, he later shied from the term Horror altogether, preferring instead "fantastique". And perhaps he was right to do so, as what he was writing from his second novel forward was no longer pure Horror but instead horror-steeped fantasy. Where his contemporaries in the genre were setting their stories wholly in the real world, Barker was building new worlds and the beings populating them were drawn as freely from dreams as they were nightmares. Barker crafted his own sort of interstitial fiction that we might today categorize as "Weird" were it marginally less popular.

Weird Fiction exists at the crossroads of the speculative fiction genres, and I differentiate it explicitly from Horror by saying that though both are concerned with the invasion of the *other* into a recognizable world, in Horror that other is malignant, whereas in Weird Fiction it isn't necessarily so. But even that fails to fully explain Weird Fiction. And that's because *Weird Fiction is, itself, other*. It's the exception to the rule. Arguably, what makes this fiction "weird" is not the content itself but how commonplace that content is. Horror is Horror because it is written with a set of tools that readers familiar with the genre recognize. Certainly, those tools and techniques shift and change over time, but what doesn't shift or change is that the readership knows they belong to "Horror". Weird, on the other hand, is *a reaction to common tools*. It's a genre of stories told in unexpected ways with uncommon combinations. By this definition Weird cannot be mainstream because the mainstream would not know how to properly decode it. Slotting Barker's work into proto-weird thus proves difficult; if there's one place Barker's work occupied, it was the mainstream. Films, books, comics, television...Barker was less author and more brand, which is what one might expect from a potential opportunist.

Is there any better example of the duality of Barker than his 1989 novel, THE GREAT AND SECRET SHOW? It starts in Omaha, Nebraska, an American town in the middle of nowhere, which echoes the popular works of Stephen King. And this isn't the only echo: the primary antagonist of THE GREAT AND SECRET SHOW is Randolph Jaffe, and it's surely no coincidence that name mirrors Randal Flagg, the villain of King's THE

STAND. Perhaps the biggest echo though is the twin metamorphoses of Jaffe into the Jaff (aligned with the dark) and Richard Wesley Fletcher into Fletcher (aligned to the light). Yin and yang. Twin antagonistic poles in conflict over the fate of the world. Or, in this case, over Quiddity, the crossroads of reality, the sea from which dreams, art, and everything else is drawn.

The metaphorical construct of Quiddity is more at home in Fantasy than in Horror; an early indicator of the direction Barker's future novels would venture. The book shows Barker at his mid-point, torn between horrors such as the Jaff's army of terata; or Kisson's Lix, snake-like creatures born of excrement and semen; and a fantastical world where lovers float upon a vast dream sea when they first lay together, and magical unseen giants occupy a misted world beyond our own. This overlap of genres is certainly *fantastique*. But is it Weird?

If, definitionally, what separates the Weird from the non-Weird is its stubborn refusal to reuse ideas that are familiar enough to have become mainstream, then how can we reconcile the notion of trying to stretch the genre to include Barker's mainstream fiction? One could argue that despite how well he fit into the milieu of twentieth century Horror, by dint of his outsider perspective (or maybe despite it) he was able to smuggle in his unconventional ideas. In essence: Weird ideas, published at a grand scale. He was ubiquitous, perhaps not so much as Stephen King, but his fame certainly extended beyond genre circles. It was shocking to see someone who, after being given access to so large a canvas, use it to deviate so confidently from the expected. Surprisingly, though, the world ended up seemingly ready for his perversities. Or, if not ready, then on the precipice of readiness. All Barker did was give them a shove.

Despite that, I don't think we can claim Barker for Weird Fiction. While it's true what he brought to mainstream Horror was unusual and discomforting, his work nevertheless bears too many hallmarks of popular fiction to truly be considered *other*. Still, Barker plays an important role in contemporary Weird Fiction. By bringing the unusual into the usual, by introducing the perverse into the conservative, Barker indelibly changed Horror fiction forever, and laid the groundwork both for the future transformations of Weird Horror, and for the subsequent evolution of Horror itself. A good number of his early readers became our foundational post-millennium Weird Fiction authors, and his prismatic influence has been reflected in their willingness to test the boundaries of what horror is and could be. Even if Barker's work cannot be considered Weird, he nevertheless helped steer the Weird ship, and made his mark on it from the outside with his outré fiction and unique imagination. And, regardless of whether he wrote Horror for the love or for the money, it's only that inspiration that truly matters.

Grey's Grotesqueries

Orrin Grey

Sucker for Mystery: The Legacy of Richard Sala

IT SEEMS that the short-lived craze of tribute anthologies is largely behind us. This is probably for the best. For a while there, it seemed like just about everyone who had a distinctive voice or a decent-sized following was getting one. But it's also a bit of a bummer, as there is at least one person who absolutely *deserves* a tribute anthology but hasn't gotten one yet.

Richard Sala is a creator whose work took some time to grow on me. I don't actually know when I first began seeing his stuff, though I remember Jesse Bullington recommending some of Sala's books to me more than a decade ago. Part of why my conversion wasn't immediate is precisely *because* Sala's style is so distinctly his own.

Combining elements of pulp magazines, old horror movies, hard-boiled detective fiction, Italian giallo, and so much more, Sala's stories inhabit a world of their own. It isn't just that his art is distinctive, it's that everything that goes on around it — from layout and lettering to the stories themselves — takes place in a world that feels at once familiar and strange.

I'm unsure precisely *what* work Sala is best known for, by those who are not devotees of his weird tales. Perhaps *Invisible Hands*, a

12-minute animated short featuring a psychic detective and a secret society of one-handed criminals, which aired in two-minute intervals on MTV's *Liquid Television* in 1991. Perhaps *The Chuckling Whatsit* or *Evil Eye*, the twelve-issue comic book series published by Fantagraphics between 1998 and 2004.

Whatever it is, and wherever you come upon it, the work of Richard Sala always feels like discovering something older, some lost treasure from the age of the pulps and yet, somehow, fiercely modern, pulling off things the pulps would never even have considered, let alone dared.

After I had become a convert to Sala's work, I was lucky enough to also become at least a friendly acquaintance, thanks to the magic of the internet. Sala had a prolific blog (https://herelies richardsala.blogspot.com/) where he published much of his artwork, and though he was relatively private about his personal life, he was active on social media, which is where I generally interacted with him. We mostly talked about old horror movies.

Sala and I shared an affection for the crime and monster movies of the first half of the 20th century. And unlike many "monster kids," Sala was as much (if not more) a fan of the Poverty Row pictures from that era as the more "classic" Universal monsters and their ilk — a fact that is probably not surprising, to those who have read his comics. Some of my favorite movies from the 1960s and before were first introduced to me thanks to conversations that we had online.

Unfortunately, Richard Sala passed away in 2020, at the age of 65. According to Wikipedia, he was felled by a heart attack, though at the time I knew only that he was gone. We were friendly, as I said, but not close enough for me to be privy to any personal details. I only knew of his passing, nothing more.

It is common, in these days of rampant social media, for us to mourn the demise of strangers whose work had an impact on our lives, even though we never knew them. I've done it myself. Few have hit me as hard as Sala's unexpected departure, however, in part because he wasn't *just* a stranger, not quite.

On the night that I first learned of his death, I watched William Castle's *The Night Walker*, in his honor. I don't know for sure if it's one of the movies he first mentioned to me or not, but it's the kind of movie he loved, and that was good enough for me.

Perhaps a better choice would have been *Doctor X*, from 1932, which might be the closest a movie has ever come to looking and feeling like a Richard Sala comic.

I started this column by suggesting that Sala deserved a tribute anthology, and I still think that's true. Sala is probably best remembered as a visual artist, and that is only right and proper, as his visual art took the forefront of his work, and is one-of-a-kind, striking, and impossible to forget. No one else was doing anything like what Sala was doing.

But unlike many creators who are known primarily as visual artists, Sala's storytelling was just as dynamic, just as striking, and, perhaps most importantly to our point here, just as *unique* as his visual art. From its subject matter and its influences to Sala's distinctive authorial voice, a Richard Sala comic was a unified experience from the words to the pictures and beyond, all capturing his skewed vision of a world filled with masked villains, secret societies, grotesque monsters, unorthodox detectives, skulking murderers, and so much more.

When a tribute anthology is published in honor of a prose author, there is always a certain amount of temptation for the stories within to become nothing more than well-meaning pastiche. Sala's style is different, however. Because he worked principally in a visual medium, it would be impossible to simulate his approach with words alone. Instead, authors who contributed to a Richard Sala tribute anthology would be forced to try to convey the unmistakable *atmosphere* of a Richard Sala comic in prose.

Maybe such an attempt would be doomed to failure. After all, as I've made clear throughout this column, no one else ever did it quite like him. But I would love to see them try... .

Black Water

Seán Padraic Birnie

My beloved, don't worry — don't move...
—William Sansom, 'A WOMAN SELDOM FOUND'

SHE WAS SITTING in one of the booths in the corner of the pub, a candle in the wine bottle before her, the tip of a cigarette glowing between her knuckles, a half pint of brown beer beside the candle. He saw her glance in his direction as the door swung shut behind him, but he honed his gaze on the bar, which glowed brightly in the dark room, lest his cheeks colour and his step falter and the ground play tricks beneath him. He took a barstool and was relieved to sit down. He smiled but the barman did not return it. Flustered and self-conscious, very tired from travel, he ordered one of the local beers, which was dark in colour and tasted, not unpleasantly, of chocolate, coffee, and old cigarettes.

He had not expected to meet someone. He had not expected that young woman to join him at the bar, nor that, minutes later, he would follow her to her booth on the other side of that dark room with low ceilings in the old town; nor that, in a few hours, she would take him to the attic she rented in a large and empty house nearby, from the skylight of which he would hear the waves breaking on a shingle beach. Nor that he would listen to those waves for months to come.

≈

THE SEA AIR, his mother had said. It'll do you good. You need to get away from things.

≈

THE HOTEL OVERLOOKED THE DOCK. On arrival an hour before he had deposited his bag in the single room, then, after making sure the door had locked, left the cramped little building and started walking without destination in mind. His journey had been long, by train, and the carriage uncomfortable, and it felt good to walk. He had slept for a small part of the duration but not so much as he had hoped. Instead his mind had drifted and he had been aware all the time of the pain in his neck and back and arms. The pain came and went. It moved about. He watched the dull countryside pass by in the dim light, the world reduced to shades of grey and hues of brown. He often felt as if he had not quite woken up: some days it was twilight all day long. He had theories about that, but the trip was supposed to take him out of that frame of mind in which he developed theories. A theory, he knew, could get you into trouble. He would have a few days to enjoy by himself, alone, then his uncle, who lived not far away, would collect him from the hotel and put him up at his farm.

Through the night he walked by the light of intermittent street-lamps. He followed narrow cobbled roads beneath the high windows of leaning houses through the old town and felt the aching of his body ease. It was a strange pain, seemingly without cause. Doctors and specialists of joint and muscle and bone had examined him without useful result. But in the rhythm of the walking he found some respite.

At the dockside he sat on a low wall and listened to the clinking of the moorings and watched the dark movement of the boats. Then he stood and stretched and decided to walk a little more, back into the old town, in search of a pub or a bar that might please him, for one drink or two.

≈

Now HE WAS LAUGHING, which came as some surprise. He felt an unexpected lightness; in her company he felt his mood lift. He had not laughed in a long time.

Oh, I have theories about that, he was saying.
About what? she asked.

The world, he said.

Don't we all, she replied.

Some people don't, he said.

They're lucky, she replied. What's your theory? she asked.

He looked at her. Her eyes were very bright in the candlelight. He wondered how much she had drunk but she was not unsteady. Her gaze was steady. She didn't seem to blink. In her brown eyes he saw his own blue gaze doubled back on him.

That none of it's real, he said. Not really.

You are aware you're not the first person to have such a thought, she said, tilting her head, smiling without smiling.

I am, he said. It's just — well, it haunts me. Sometimes. I can't explain it.

I know the feeling, she said.

You do? he asked.

Oh yes, she said. I mean, the world is extraordinary. Just the fact of it. That anything should exist. It beggars belief.

He expected her to proceed but she did not, though she continued to nod, staring down at the table. Then she clicked her neck, turning her head at an angle.

So, he said. I've told you all about me. How about you? Where are you from?

Nowhere interesting, she said. Nowhere at all, really.

No one's from nowhere, he replied. He had tried to place her accent but had failed: at first he had thought she was from the south, that she came from a family with means, but he was no longer so sure.

She finished her drink. I am, she said.

He frowned.

Well? she said. Are we going?

He felt such abandon in this moment — such sudden freedom, such joy in life.

THE ATTIC ROOM was large and plain. A mattress lay under the slant of the ceiling on one side, and a large window opened out onto the night. Since his arrival in town a fresh wind had gathered its strength and he could hear the sound of it through the skylight and the ceiling, through the insulation and the roof tiles above and through the chimney. With nowhere else to put it he set the bottle of wine down on the floor, then placed his coat, neatly folded, beside it.

My landlady is hardly ever here, said his companion. Most of the rooms are empty. Sometimes I think I live alone.

Have you been here long? he asked, wondering how long someone might live in a place and it remain so bare of clutter and decoration.

A few months, she replied. The person I came here to meet never showed up.

I'm sorry, he said, wondering what else to say.

She turned around. It's not a bad thing, she said, smiling without smiling. I found you. Then she kissed him.

As if a kiss were a body of dark water into which a person might fall.

Have we met before? he asked.

Don't be ridiculous, she said.

Are you sure? he asked, kissing her neck.

Shut up, she said.

She unclipped first one buckle and then the next of the russet pinafore, then kicked off her shoes, flats, which clattered against the skirting board. With unexpected strength she moved him toward the window. It occurred to him that he was very drunk. The wind buffeted the glass, which shook in its frame. He felt the house moving like an old ship and thought of the clinking of the dark boats on the water. He was sitting on the low wall, breathing the sea air. He was on a train passing through dull countryside comprised of hues of grey and shades of brown. He was putting his bag down in a lonely hotel room — then he was here and she was unbuttoning the buttons of his shirt.

Lie down, she said.

She kissed him, then pushed him down by one shoulder.

Careful, he said, laughing.

Shut up, she whispered, and kissed him again.

Then he started to gag. At first it hurt — he felt a scalding, the presence of something unexpectedly solid. But then, from that scalding, he felt a sensation not unpleasurable fan out. Her lips tightened over his own. She pressed down on him. He was suddenly sleepy; he felt the strength depart his body, felt his muscles relax. He might have been seated in a dentist's chair. That residue of pain which never left him began to leave him. He felt that thing pushing down through his throat. Though numbed he felt its slow movement inside him. He could not breathe but did not panic. As if she might breathe for the two of them. There was no reason to panic. She is feeding me, he thought, like a goose. To fatten me up. The thought did not trouble him. Now that thing was in his chest; now he felt it enter his stomach, probing, reaching. For a moment he regarded the procedure with some curiosity. Then he was gone, lost to sensation, under the spell of the night.

HE AWOKE NAUSEOUS, in new pain, without memory beyond his own gaze doubled back in her eyes; candlelight; dark beer and an unsmiling barman in a pub that was empty beyond the young woman alone in one booth. He tried to speak.

Don't worry yourself, she said.

He was very hot. The sheets were sodden. She placed a cool flannel on his forehead.

Don't worry, she said. You need to rest. There's no reason to worry.

THE PAIN EBBED. She must have replaced the sheets while he slept. He lacked energy to a degree he had never known before: he felt the lack of it pressing down on him. He watched her walking about the room. She went in circles, head bowed, lips moving. She stood smoking beneath the open window, watching him. Her eyes were very large and brown, her black hair pulled back from her face in a ponytail. He could hear the wind at the window.

She brought him water. She brought him food but he could not eat. He slept.

HE AWOKE IN THE NIGHT, crying out. She held him.

It's okay, she said. There's no reason to worry.

~

HIS BODY WAS CHANGING. Time beyond his grasp of it was passing. A new pain, unlike any pain he had known, bloomed in his stomach.

His belly began to swell.

What's happening? he asked, his voice hoarse from disuse.

It won't be long, she said.

~

HE AWOKE INFLAMED, his belly engorged. He pushed the sheets away. His belly red and swollen and gigantic. He felt movement within him, as of a shoal of small fish.

In his dream he had screamed at her: let me out. In his dream such madness as this could not possibly be. In his dream the world still belonged to a rational order of things, things out of which ordinary sense might be made. Waking each time the madness of it shocked him afresh.

The world beyond the room was a dream. A hotel, a train journey, an uncle, a mother — such things had ceased to mean very much. Every day his memories faded. He could not remember his own name nor the name of his companion nor the name of the town. Did such a place truly exist? It could not. There was only the plain room, the floorboards, the window. The pane of glass rattling in its frame. When she opened the window, the sea air, sailing into the room. The damp rot of a building close to water. The little dock and the beach. A strange euphoria, borne of the pain.

~

THROUGH THE LONG hours she tended him. She lay next to him on the mattress unsleeping. She massaged his shoulders and whispered in his ear. She kissed his neck as he stared up at the window, his eyes filmed and red. His coat, neatly folded, lay on the floor. Beside it stood a bottle of wine, unopened.

∼

ONE MORNING he awoke and he saw them, teeming inside him. His belly translucent now, flesh like dull glass: through that dim translucency he saw *eyes* flitting through a flowing substance akin to smoke or black water. As he stared at the eyes they gazed back at him.

I think I'm ready, he said.

∼

A MEMORY: the young man was on a train, coming from where he did not know, going where he did not know. His body in pain. He was trying to sleep. In the shallows of sleep he dreamt of winding streets of high buildings and of a pub nestled in darkness and in one booth of the pub a candle, glowing, stuck in an old bottle of wine.

∼

WILL IT HURT? he asked.

Yes, it will hurt, she said.

Will you be with me? he asked, holding her hand as the pain began to flow.

Of course I'll be with you, she said, smiling without smiling. Of course.

New in Town

Corey Farrenkopf

I.

THERE IS a crypt in the cemetery in the center of town. There is someone inside the crypt. Everyone in town knows who's inside the crypt, but they won't tell you. No name is written on the outside of the crypt. Just a date and a once-ornate angel with most of her details worn smooth with age. You are new in town. Your neighbors refuse to call you neighbor…not until you enter the crypt. Until you come out of the crypt. That is, if you come out of the crypt. They don't tell you what happens if you don't or if that's a possibility in the first place. You can tell by the tone of their voices that it is definitely a possibility, but you don't ask further questions. It's a rite of passage, so you stand on the moss-speckled marble steps, staring down into what you believe will become the burial chamber, waiting to meet whoever lies below. The town is a desirable place to call home. There aren't many of those anymore, so you take the first step into the damp subterranean air.

II.

There is a little free library in front of your house. You can't miss the shrunken glass door or the little mock shingles or the folk-art marigolds painted on the sides. The structure was there when you bought the place, still stocked with best sellers and children's picture books, Sci-fi novels and some raunchy smut. You scan through the titles until you find a handwritten notebook. There is something dried on the pages, coffee brown. The substance sticks to your fingertips as you scan through, trying to decipher the words within. There are no spaces between the words. Each crashes into the next, a single run-on sentence across 120 pages. *Therearethe-breathsinthenighttherearethebreathsinthedaytherearethebreaths*... Nothing but pleading dread. There is a stretch of pages that grow illegible, consonant combinations that refuse to align, too many vowels pushed together in O-heavy formations. You can barely read it, but the last page is clean and clear, as if intentional. There is a name, a phone number, a dollar value listed as a reward. Would the reward be the money, or the knowledge, or the alleviation of the pleading dread that has seeped from the book into your chest? You don't know, but your phone is in your hand, the number on the screen, the dial tone droning in your ear.

III.

There is a tent in the woods behind your home. At least you think it is a tent. It is strung up between two oaks, synthetic (organic?) fabric shivering in the wind. You never saw who put it up, or if it was already there when you moved into your new home. Moss grows on the sides and drapes in wispy beards over the entrance flap. At night you hear the zippered doorway unzip, the sound sharp like sudden birdsong through a pine grove. Sometimes there are footsteps in the undergrowth. Sometimes there is stillness. You cannot bring yourself to investigate. You tell yourself they will move on soon enough. Why hassle someone who may or may not be going through a rough time? Because, let's be honest, you don't even know if the tent is on your property. Boundary lines have always been vague in your opinion. You start to find trinkets on your back porch on nights when the zipper cuts through your quiet evenings. Medallions woven of bittersweet vines, owl pellets bloated with bone, strips of hair woven into elegant knots. You don't like the gifts, so you leave the floodlights on every night, hoping to deter your neighbor/squatter/unseen friend from depositing anything else on your steps. But the tent keeps unzipping and the gifts keep appearing: stones etched with elongated faces, acorns stuffed into canning jars, a knife with a rust-rimmed blade. The last gives you the most anxiety, as if all the rest hadn't already caused your heart to skip against your ribs. In some ways it seems like a solution. You can return the gift. Tell whoever is living in the tent *No Thank You/I Don't Take Kindly To Threats.* And if they don't get the gesture, you have other options. It is a knife after all. Who's to say that isn't what your neighbor/squatter/unseen friend wants? You only give gifts you hope will be useful someday.

∿

IT's hard to move to a new town. It's hard to integrate into an existing community. It's hard to leave everything you are comfortable with behind, trading it in for the unknown, the veiled and secreted, the splendid and the wondrous. We understand. We do. It's just tradition. You will see. We promise. This is the best place in the world to live. The best place for you. We welcome everyone with open arms, but only if...

I.

There is a stone casket inside the crypt inside the cemetery at the center of town. You're surprised at how far down the steps take you into the burial chamber. It feels like you have been walking for hours, down and down and down, until you are miles beneath town, but you know that can't be right, structurally speaking anyway. Who had the ability to tunnel like this back in the 1700s? The dates on the mausoleum's wall told you as much, when the body was interred, the crypt erected. Yet here you are, where your neighbors told you to be if you ever wanted to use the pickleball courts, or the weightroom in the community center, or the lap pool/spa/sauna, or the nature trails that run alongside the reservoir. It's so cold. Gooseflesh covers your arms and neck. You would have worn a jacket if you knew it would be like this. You would have done many things differently if you knew it was going to be like this. You'd seen all the pictures on Instagram, the autumnal foliage during fall, the quaint snow-covered downtown sidewalks in winter. You read somewhere that three of the top ten most photographed places in America were within the town borders. And for some reason, that spoke to you, whispered in your ear that you no longer wanted to live where you'd been living for the past fifteen years. Change is necessary for growth, for happiness, for you to become the person you always meant to be, because, let's be honest, you were never very content with your lot in life, your underwhelming job, your bland family, your three cats that never give you the time of day and insist on spraying your side of the bed every chance they get. That's all behind you now, because you are standing over the rough-hewn casket in the center of the earth, peering down at the person/thing/god??? that will allow you to become who you always wanted to become. The lid is only open a crack and a voice at the back of your head tells you to remove it, put all your strength into lifting the cover to truly see who's gifts you are about to receive.

III.

There is a child inside a sleeping bag inside the tent behind your house. Or maybe they are a teenager, or a twenty-something. You have always been bad with ages. You unzipped the flap, knife raised, to find them slumbering, warm fur-lined fabric pulled up to their chin. There is a crown of woven twigs circling their reclined head, dried berries dangling from the vines. They do not stir. You call into the tent, a quiet introduction that grows to a calling alarm as the child/teen/twenty-something slumbers on. You have so many questions for them. About the gifts. The acorns and totems. The knife. The knife is the biggest question of all. Is it a threat? A preparation? A way out? You ask them again and again, but they remain still. This town was supposed to be quaint and safe. But this though — this was not what you saved up that massive downpayment for. Something is off about the tent's interior. It might be the smell, dank with rot, sweet like wine. The temperature within is sweltering compared to outside. It's like the greenhouse at the arboretum in the town you used to live in. You stick your arm inside, but are unsure if you can proceed. You've always been told to leave the sleeping...or maybe those that sleepwalk? It's rude to wake them. But the knife, but the gifts, but your property line. They have no right to be sleeping where they are, and you'll tell them as much once you wake them. A shake should pull them from dreams, just two hands on their shoulders, a sudden jerk, and their eyes will open. You are sure of this, just as you are sure this is your home and they don't belong here, no matter how long their tent has been pitched by the back corner of your property.

II.

There is a church next to the coffee shop in the center of town. Steeple white, stained-glass crimson. The man on the other end of the phone says that's where you'll meet, that he is the pastor for their small congregation, that everyone in town has read the notebook at one time or another and always felt the need to return it to its author. *But are you its author?* you ask before the line goes dead. *No I am not*, the pastor replies before hanging up. *We are all the author.* And this strikes you as odd, but you've never been the religious type, so maybe he means it in a more communal way than your mind wants to imagine, one hand being all hands and such. You stand before the white steeple, notebook sealed in a plastic ziplock bag. The pages were beginning to smell of rot. You couldn't just leave it on the car seat as you drove. Smells don't fade. You worry about a lingering stain. The pastor waits for you on the front steps, black cassock and white collar as the movies prepared you for. He waves. You approach and exchange small talk, continually trying to hand the ziplocked book to the man, but he refuses to take it, talking on and on about the town, and how glad he is that you've moved in, and how glad he is that you've found the book, as everyone has found the book, and that you felt compelled to call. *Can you just take it?* You eventually ask, exasperated. You have things to do. Errands. Groceries. Pilates at two. *The book can only change hands inside the chapel*, the pastor replies. *Follow me. We need to see if you'll join the congregation. Now is the time to decide.* Religion has always seemed cultish to you, but you can't just say that to a man who's dedicated his life to the idea, and you are polite, so you don't argue, though you know what your answer will be.

...THEY ARE willing to open to us. Open their hearts and minds, their eyes and ears and throats, and wallets, on occasion, but only on occasion, we promise. Open in all the ways that matter is what we are trying to say. We will be open with you. How can you expect us not to desire reciprocation? We would never put you in harm's way. Never...not unless you refuse to be open. This community has thrived on openness for hundreds of years. We can't have that withering with each new neighbor we welcome. Call it a test. Call it tradition. Call it the true meaning of home.

I.

There is a body in the casket in the crypt in the cemetery at the center of the town. The body belongs to the town's founder, a man you picture in pilgrim garb, ill kept beard and smallpox scarred face. The metal plate hammered into the stone next to the coffin says as much, illuminated by your cell phone light, almost as if this is a museum piece. You search for an artist statement, but find none. The body of the town's founder lies inside, arms crossed over his chest, skin the texture of leather pulled taut over skull and rib. No one gave you instructions on what to do once you met the founder. No offering was suggested, no item to be retrieved or riddle to answer. You search the surrounding claustrophobic space with your light, hunting for an instruction manual of some sort, even a stretch of poorly carved hieroglyphics you can puzzle out, but there is nothing. There are also no piles of bone heaped about, so that's promising. You scroll through the reel of your memories, searching for a touchstone, some flicker of insight on what to do when you come upon a being in a tomb. You've watched a lot of horror movies and fairytale retellings. There has to be something there. Think harder. Try to connect the dots. Your mind only circles *Sleeping Beauty*, again and again. It's a similar scenario, minus the beauty, and the sleeping; though, if you think about it, death is kind of like sleeping...eternal slumber and all that, and you have no better idea, so you bend at the waist over the edge of the casket and plant your lips on the leathered forehead of the town's founder praying he will accept you. You press them there for a moment, waiting for some key to turn inside an invisible lock. There is a moment when you think you should lean back, that maybe the lack of consent was a bad idea, that you should have asked permission from the founder to join his town, but then the hands are upon you, skeletal fingers dragging you into the casket, towards the skull, jaw distending, wider and wider and wider. There should be a fossilized throat before you, a paper-thin windpipe. There is none of that. In fact, what lies before you, inside the founder's mouth, the space where you are being slowly dragged, is another cavern much like the one you are currently falling from, only much larger, and filled with writhing bodies. You try to grab on to the casket's edge, but the stone is smooth, and you lose your grip. You tumble into the founder's mouth, flailing through the air until your body becomes one with the crowd below, the crowd that lives inside the founder's chest. You knew things were too simple. You knew social media never painted an accurate portrait of anything. You knew that you should have just been content with your lackluster life and your three spray-happy cats, but no, now you have all eternity to look forward to in an old man's gullet, buried in a crypt in the cemetery at the center of the town for which the man gave a name. You can't remember the name anymore. You're not sure you ever really did.

III.

There are flecks of gold in the child/teen/twenty-something's otherwise all-devouring black eyes. Your hands are on their shoulders, knife discarded to the side of the sleeping bag sewn of animal hide. At first you thought it was store bought, now, up close, you can tell it is hand stitched, the carcasses of a dozen different species woven together with rough thread. The child/teen/twenty-something stares up at you and you no longer have any doubt about their age. Youth slips away with consciousness. The being lying before you is ancient, withered, hundreds of years sweeping over their skin. You stammer an apology, lips fumbling over words, and this makes the person's smile broaden, revealing mismatched teeth, as if each belonged to another's mouth. You scream and reach for the knife, but before your hand can find the hilt, the ancient child/teen/twenty-something's hand reaches up and caresses your face, fingernail tracing the edge of your jaw. You lose your balance and tumble down next to them, unable to move your limbs, your mouth no longer spitting out words, paralysis sweeping through your veins. You try to struggle as the crowned being slips from the sleeping bag, revealing their skin stitched together from the skin of others, much like the bag itself, but naked to the waist. They peel back the fabric from their sleeping bag and gently roll you inside, snuggling the hides around your neck, tucking you in like your mother had done all those years ago. They nudge a sweat-soaked pillow beneath your head, the smells of rot and stagnation sharp and overwhelming, but there is nothing you can do. Your body betrays you. Before the sewn being steps from the tent, they bend once more, removing the crown of bittersweet from their head and place it upon yours. Then they slip from the tent, zipping you inside, giving you peace and quiet so you may sleep. And it's then that you realize all you ever wanted to do was sleep, sleep for ages. You don't care about the new house in the highly desirable town, or the mortgage you had to take out to get here. All you care about is the blanket of furs, the shivering fabric overhead, the warmth settling into your bones. It was a gift after all, and gifts are always meant to be useful.

II.

There are parishioners lining the pews inside the chapel in the center of town, Sunday best buttoned up to their throats, billowing dresses that look homespun, ties coarse and of natural hues. Each head swivels in your direction at the creek of the massive wooden doors. They smile at you. They wave. They are the people you've seen at the grocery store, or at Pilates, or at any of the dozen places where your errands take you. But it isn't Sunday. Parishes hold mass on other days, you tell yourself. Once you step over the threshold, you jab the ziplocked book at the pastor, nudging him in the shoulder, insisting he take it off your hands. You can't bear to hold the book anymore. It shivers beneath your touch, a low humming drone slipping from beneath the cover, that winding voice winding once more through the nearly endless sentence. *Therearethebreathsinthenighttherearethebreathsinthedaytherearethebreaths...*
The pastor only smiles, letting you attempt to stab him with the notebook's blunt edges. *Now it is time to breathe with us. Respiration is key to well-being to becoming one with your neighbors.* You tell him you aren't interested in becoming "one" with your neighbors, that you

just wanted to give the book back, that you have places to go and people to see, but he won't hear of it. When you throw the book down the central aisle of the church, a young woman leaves her pew and picks it up as the pastor slips in front of the door, blocking your exit. *People move to our town for the air. For the community. You are no different.* Then there are hands on your shoulders. Two men in matching blue suits lead you to the front of the chapel, to a seat painted in gold leaf, a lectern off to one side, bare of adornment. They guide you, like sheep dogs to a flock, nudging you towards the chair, towards the lectern. When you drop into the seat, the young woman unzips the plastic and places the notebook on the lectern, peeling apart the pages until it is splayed before you, the run-on sentence nearly chanting in your ears. At first you think you are hallucinating, then you look out over the gathered congregation, and their lips are moving, the words from the book sweeping up around your ears, hurried and propulsive. Your eyes follow along, the young woman turning the pages. Before you know it, your lips are moving too, tongue unwinding around each consonant and vowel, speaking in time with the congregation, the words tunneling through your brain, etching deep grooves into your gray matter. It almost feels like the words have always been there, or like you've always been searching for them, for this place, for this community. Religion has never been your thing, but you are amenable to change. Rigidity is never something you want people to associate you with. You want to breathe the air. You want to share the words. You want to know what the rest know. You want and you want and you want and you will have, or so says the pastor, speaking right into your ear as you take the book into your lap, turning the pages on your own. You were always meant to change the pages. And you were always meant to replace the book in the Little Free Library at the edge of your property once you are done, once the sentence has been spoken, because there will always be someone new in town, and they, too, will need to read the words. You will be waiting in your own pew for when the time comes.

~

NOT EVERYONE IS MEANT for our community. Not everyone can be a perfect fit. You know that now. But you also know you are one of us. You have always been one of us. You are no longer new in town. Not after what you've gone through, what you've seen and achieved. This is home. This is what you've always wanted. Community. Acceptance. A sense of oneness, of openness, of joy. You are welcome. We are glad you are here.

It Knows What's Under Your Skin

Jason Fernandes

I watch your arrival from the monitors in the dressing room. You show up twenty minutes late, just as our system predicted. You creep along the cobblestone path, head already swiveling, ready for anything that might jump out at you.

Tyler trudges behind you, hands spilling out of his too-tight jean pockets. He's only here because of you, because of your "weird obsession with dark shit," as he put it in a text to his friend. He doesn't know we've been reading his texts. Neither do you, for that matter.

"Kir, wait up," he calls to you.

Our mics feed us the squishy patter of your sneakers, your quick, shallow breaths. Tyler gives us a slower, two-part thud with each footfall, followed by the faint scrape of his high-tops dragging on the stone.

I walk back and forth in the dressing room, dragging my feet hard on the linoleum, trying to scuff my own shoes to replicate what looks like weeks of abuse on his. You probably won't notice a detail like this, but nailing the details is what sets us apart.

I do a final review of our data scrape. Tyler: 27-year-old private equity associate, early childhood attachment issues, fear of abandonment. The type of rich kid we love scaring the shit out of. You:

28-year-old software engineer, mother died when you were nine, fear of death and depersonalization. We know more about you and Tyler than you know about each other. We know, for instance, that you had an affair with a colleague named Wyatt that you never told Tyler about. We know Tyler's been hiding a minor coke habit from you. It's all there, in the data you let us access when you signed the waivers.

You knock on the front door. We don't answer until we can get a close-up of Tyler from the doorbell camera.

As soon as he catches up to you, we snap the photo, and the makeup artists surround me, making their final adjustments.

We usually start our guests off with the more conventional stuff: walls that close in, jump-scares, darkness. You've never considered yourself afraid of the dark, but you haven't experienced true darkness, the kind that suffocates, the kind that begins to feel more internal than external. The kind of darkness that conceals a face six inches in front of your own.

You'll encounter that in the second room.

But the first scare for you comes in the entryway. While our manager is reminding you of the house rules, you notice a framed photo behind her, a photo whose significance only you understand. It's a photo of Wyatt, holding a cocktail and smiling at you, the unseen photographer. (You've never shared this photo with anyone, and you deleted it shortly after you took it. But we still have access to it, and we know what it means to you). I watch your reaction on the monitors. You do a literal double-take, then you try to swallow your reaction so as not to alert Tyler.

The makeup artists finish as you enter the first room. I look at myself in the mirror to admire their work. I roll my shoulders forward and lift my nose into a slight sneer to accentuate the likeness.

"Kirsten, hey, Kir," I say, practicing Tyler's drawl.

I continue to watch your progress, waiting for my moment to enter.

You and Tyler have left the second room, and you now face two doors, both slightly ajar, one labeled, "Kirsten," the other, "Tyler." It's too dark to see what lies beyond either threshold. You start walking toward yours.

"Fuck that, I'm going with you," Tyler says, fighting to keep the fear out of his voice.

"Wait," you tell him. "This is all part of it. We should do it."

Tyler hesitates; he clearly doesn't want to be left alone in this place. But before he can mount an argument, you've already given him a peck on the cheek and left him for the next room. We close and lock the door behind you, so he no longer has the option to follow you.

The furnaces have been raging in Tyler's room. Taking his jacket is easy: he removes it almost instantly to cope with the heat, and while he searches for an exit, I slip in and out undetected.

Armed with Tyler's jacket — and his scent — I hurry off to meet you.

I watch you enter the fifth room. It's an exact replica of your childhood bedroom, down to the faded photographs of a once-happy family. I imagine your awe at our handiwork, the slow questioning of your reality. By now, you're probably opening the diary hidden inside the hollowed-out dictionary on your bookshelf. How could we have known?

On every page of the diary is a single sentence, scrawled in the shaky lettering of your youth: *I think Daddy is going to kill Mommy.*

You run out into the hall and slam the door behind you. The hall is much darker than the room you just left; you do not see me at first.

I slouch and tremble. I pretend my excitement is fear. I am Tyler.

"Kir?" I say. "Kirsten?"

"Ty?"

"I'm here," I say, reaching out a hand for you.

You take my hand. Our fingers fall into place as though they've done this a thousand times before. I give your hand a small squeeze, imputing the gesture with as much love as I believe Tyler is capable of. You squeeze my hand in return.

The final room is meant to appear to you as a compendium of personal horrors: dysmorphic mirrors, grating sounds, objects that remind you of your mother's death. But now that I'm with you, you're no longer frightened. You lean your head on my shoulder.

"I love you," I say.

The final door lies ahead of us, beneath a glowing exit sign that promises to return you to your world.

I push open the door, and we're immediately greeted by the sensations of the evening. Cool air wraps itself around us; cars and cicadas buzz with delightful mundanity. I can feel the tension leave your body.

Hand in hand, we walk into the night.

Homunculus

Derrick Boden

DEAR ALEX,

I shouldn't be writing you. Not ever, but especially not here, not now. The doctors said it. My therapist said it. Hell, I said it. The psychological consequences of reengaging with you, my better half, would be unpredictable. Severe. We're our own people now, with our own lives. There's no reason to pick at wounds long healed. And yet, from the moment Sumaira and I rounded the bend on Route 1 and Deer Fly Island came into view, I knew I would write this letter.

Someday, I might even send it.

It was a long drive up from Boston. Our asses were sore from the sitting, our tongues worn out from the sniping. Ripley barked at every fucking car from Portland to the Deer Fly bridge. Would've been idyllic, winding our way up the coast with the dog at the kennel. But lo, Sumaira says the Inn is pet friendly, so here we are.

It feels unnatural, coming back after all this time. Like squinting through a haze that no one else can see. What about you? I bet you visit all the time. What's it like, hiking these old trails? Can you feel Mom's hand around ours? Can you hear Dad fret as we veer off the trail, on the hunt for another grub-infested fairy house? I can.

Even if it isn't my hand.

I took us off the paved road, along the bluffs that overlook the tide pools. We counted a dozen, whorling with froth and deceptively deep. A decrepit motorboat banged against the rocks a ways up. I told Sumaira how they lose a tourist every season to the riptide, their heads dashed against the barnacle-crusted rocks, their bodies washed ashore on the mainland a week later all bulging and blue.

"Trying to scare me?" she said.

"Maybe."

She doesn't know about us. She's in med school for psychiatry. She's an eager student. It would be a disaster if she ever found out.

Mr. Almandine, a tall man with soft hands and a hard stare, showed us to our room. I don't remember him from before, but not much else has changed. The carpets, once expensive, have worn thin. The brass sconces are tarnished, the windows thicker at the bottom where the glass has settled. It even smells the same, I think — musty with a hint of stale pine — though I can't trust my nose since the procedure.

"I should formally invite you to our dining room." Mr. Almandine's baritone was smooth and toneless: Marvin Gaye reciting Gregorian chants. "From six o'clock."

The way he worded it, I couldn't tell if he was in fact inviting us to dinner. I waited for him to say more. He did not. Ripley licked his knuckles greedily. Eventually, we thanked the man and wheeled our luggage inside. But Mr. Almandine kept standing there. He watched me fuck with the latch on my suitcase. His smile seemed forced, contrite. As if one of us had committed a terrible sin.

"Oh, right." I pried my wallet from my pocket, pulled out a five. "Here."

Mr. Almandine stared at the money in horror. "Oh, no. I cannot."

Chastened, I pocketed the cash. Mr. Almandine still didn't leave. Eventually, with no other choice, I shut the door — though it couldn't have been six inches from his face. I pressed my ear to the door. I could hear him breathing, haltingly.

It was a full minute before he padded away.

Sumaira came in from the balcony. "What a view! I — what is it?"

I bolted the door. "Nothing."

Behind her, a pair of deer flies buzzed in on a swell of warm, muggy air. I remembered what they felt like crawling on my forearm. Your forearm. I remember them bearing down, gnashing in. The flush of pain, the swell of blood, the itch we'd scratch at for so long it would leave a scar. Standing there, today, I ran my hand down my smooth, unblemished forearm and thought of you.

Then I killed the flies with my shoe and shut the balcony door.

Yours,
Ander

~

Dear Alex,

I should clarify. I am not jealous. The fact that you kept our body, it was purely a medical decision. Your hemisphere was in better shape, they said. Give the best chance to the strongest contestant. That I am even here today — the leftover, the left, the homunculus — is both a marvel and a miracle.

While Sumaira unpacked, I sat on the balcony and penned my first letter to you. By the end of it, I knew it wouldn't be the last. What a fool I must be, to think you'll one day take interest in this drivel.

On our way to the elevator, we were waylaid by a woman in a vintage apron vacuuming the hall. She was facing us, had to have seen us — yet she showed no intention of stopping, nor even moving aside for us to pass. Sumaira had insisted we get gussied up for dinner, despite the remoteness of this place, and now I tried to keep a distance between my leather shoes and the hungering vacuum. It was an obscenely powerful model, pulverizing lost buttons, devouring the husks of dead deer flies and fetal-curled spiders. Sumaira edged left, then right. The woman ceded no ground. In fact, it was she who was driving us back with relentless thrusts of her mongrel machine.

Eventually, I shouted, "Excuse me!"

The woman seemed to look straight through us. She said noth-ing. The vacuum reared in her hard-knuckled grip, clipped my toe. I leapt backward, grabbed Sumaira's hand and made for the stairs at the opposite end of the hall.

"Weird fucking place," I said as we entered the dining room at last.

The host led us to our table. Sumaira shrugged, the way she does when she thinks I'm being square. "*I* think it's charming."

"Go feed *your* footwear to that witch's vacuum, then."

She studied my face. "This place brings back memories."

"No." I've told her about weekending up here as a child. She knows Mom and Dad are dead. "You know, every conversation doesn't have to be a therapy session."

She looked out the window, trying to keep the frustration from reaching her face. I'll be honest, things haven't been great for some time.

"Sorry," I said. "I'm just...it was a long drive."

The waiter set two sweating glasses of water on our table. Between the glasses, I had a clear view to the opposite side of the room. The shock ripped through me like a chainsaw through cheesecloth. I gulped at the air. I must've reached for my glass, must've missed. Ice water soiled the tablecloth, the carpet. The waiter backpedaled right onto the fallen glass. It crunched like bone filigree. Everyone stopped — words choked off mid-sentence, forks hovering at parted lips — and stared.

Everyone except you.

The silence lingered, a communal embarrassment. A dozen conversations lurched awkwardly forward. I offered to help with the mess, but Mr. Almandine was there, from nowhere, waving me off while the waiter swept mangled glass teeth into a metal dustpan.

Sumaira said something. You rose from your seat, thanked the host, and left for the hotel proper. I watched the casual ease of your gait. The lazy, confident slouch. The crooked curve of your lips. I was appalled, enrapt. In your movements I saw myself, distorted through time. I saw perfection in your smile.

My smile.

Your smile.

I shouldn't be here. But now I know I cannot leave.

Yours,
Ander

～

Dear Alex,

Slept like shit. The window AC unit wheezed out nothing but hot air, so we left the window open instead. A deer fly burrowed through the screen. It buzzed to the clock, then to the closet, then back. Every time I started to drift off, it buzzed another lap. I couldn't inhale without imagining the thing crawling down my windpipe. I gave up at dawn, rooted around the room for a coffee maker until Ripley woke up and growled.

"Hmn?" Sumaira sat up. Her eyes were still closed, nightgown sliding off her shoulder. "What time is it?"

"Too early." There was no coffee maker. "Gonna see if the cafe is open."

"Take the dog," she mumbled.

Downstairs, Mr. Almandine (who clearly never sleeps) waved cordially from his expansive lacquer concierge desk. "Sleep well, I presume?"

The morning crew were still setting up breakfast, but they'd put out an urn of dark roast. I've had worse. Through the foyer window, in the parking lot, there you were. Tossing a handsome roller bag into the trunk of a black Audi two-door.

I drained the coffee in three scalding gulps and stepped outside.

When you looked up, you smiled as if you'd been expecting me.

I tied Ripley to the bike rack. He let out a throaty growl. He's never liked me. "Hey. I...I'm Ander."

"I know." Of course you knew. You had your jacket slung over your shoulder. Neither of us offered a hand to shake. "Enjoying your stay?"

It was a banal thing for you to ask. But what was there to say? You knew everything about me, the past five years notwithstanding. My mind was a castoff, my body a second-hand thing. Not like yours.

Regardless, I saw your hand. Like mine, it was trembling.

"Just arrived," I said.

You motioned to your car. "Damn, just leaving. I have a conference..."

Up close, I noticed things. The way you moved, it wasn't quite the same. Five years is a long time. What have you been up to in our body? Regrettable things? The car is a rental. There's a police scanner on the dash.

"Of course," I said. "This is my first time back."

"I come every summer."

"Keeping up the family tradition?" I tried to laugh, but it didn't sound like me — and besides, it wasn't funny. You winced. Absurdly, I thought about the seizures. Do you remember what the doctors told us after the accident? They said our brain was attacking itself. Our corpus callosum, the bridge between our two cerebral hemispheres, had sustained irreparable damage. One half of our brain would eventually kill the other half.

When I saw you wince, do you know what I thought? I thought: what if my brain had reached across the dew-damp asphalt and seized yours?

"Something like that," you said.

Embarrassed, I felt compelled to prove my own commitment to our family. This, despite having walked — having *been directed* — away from them years ago. "I visit their graves twice a year. On birthdays."

You nodded. "That's nice."

"I've seen you there, once or twice." I regretted saying it. "I wait until you're gone. You know, to respect your privacy."

You nodded, as if you understood. Which I doubt. You kept the family name, after all. You kept everything.

"We should catch up sometime." You glanced at your car, shot me that look we always used when we were ready to bail on an awkward conversation.

"Of course, right. So long."

I started to extend my hand. You flinched back. I made myself smile, apologetically. I get it. I wouldn't want to touch me, either.

On my way inside, I glanced up. Sumaira was standing at the window of our room, in her nightgown, staring down. I waved. Only then did I realize that she wasn't looking at me.

Yours,
Ander

~

Dear Alex,

Sumaira wanted to take it easy our first full day on the island. I suspect she said this for my benefit, because of the incident at dinner. This made me irritable, but she's right. We have all week. It's a small island. There's nowhere to go.

She left for the market with Ripley while I was showering. The room was still empty when I got out. As I was toweling off, I heard her laugh. She has a very distinctive laugh. I crept to the window — why I crept, I cannot say — and looked down on the parking lot.

You were there at your car, as if you'd never left. Only, you had your sleeves rolled up past the elbows and the top two buttons of your shirt undone. Your triangle of exposed chest glistened with sweat in the hard morning light. The hood of your car was propped open; a wrench lay on the asphalt nearby. You were saying something to Sumaira, who leaned against your car with her hips outthrust, the way a model might pose to wait for a hypothetical bus. The bag of groceries at her feet was an afterthought. Ripley chased grasshoppers through the grass.

You wiped grease from your hands with a rag, said something I couldn't hear. Sumaira laughed again. It was a big, easy laugh. I hadn't heard it in a while. It did something unpleasant to my gut.

I kept watching.

You said something else, shrugged. Sumaira gave you a playful shove. Ripley bounded up, attacked your hand with long lashes from his tongue. A deer fly landed on my arm, and only then did I realize I was still in my towel, crouched low at the window so as not to be seen. The deer fly picked its way through my arm hair, to the exact spot where we'd been bit as a child. I flinched and it bit me. I killed it, left a greasy burgundy smear down my arm. Outside, Mr. Almandine had arrived to offer assistance. On her way back inside, Sumaira glanced over her shoulder in a way that made you smile.

I was suddenly overcome with shame, though I can't say why.

The conversation was far from private. Still, it felt like I'd been spying on a couple in the shower. I quickly got dressed, had just looped my belt when Sumaira opened the door.

She took one look at me and said, "You're bleeding."

"Bug bite." I shrugged, though in truth it stung badly. "Who was that?"

I hadn't meant to bring you up.

"His name is Alex," she said, and she was glowing.

I thought he was leaving, I almost said. "Car trouble?"

"Yeah." Ripley darted through her legs, growled at me half-heartedly and made for the balcony. "Spark plug or something. Concierge is gonna call a mechanic."

At night, to my surprise, Sumaira slid into bed naked. When she lowered herself onto me, her thighs trembled. She came quickly, fiercely, her head thrust back. Her eyes were closed, like she was dreaming. Or trying to. She moaned a word, softly, but I couldn't make it out. In the desk lamp, I caught a glimpse of my reflection.

It was you.

Regards,
Ander

∿

ALEX,

This morning, Sumaira wanted to check out the lighthouse. I've seen that movie, no thank you. Besides, the flies were back last night and I slept like shit again (upon giving up, I penned my most recent letter in the turbid hours before dawn). I was irritable, and eventually I'd say something regrettable. At least she took the dog. After she left, I packed a sandwich and went for a hike to clear my mind.

Not my best idea.

The fairy houses are still there. I'm sure you know. I don't know what I was expecting to find. Tranquility, maybe. Memories take on a strange shape, when left to fester in the dark. I thought my childhood imagination had exaggerated the houses, made them bigger, weirder, more haunting. If anything, it was the opposite.

The first house I spotted was just off the trail. It was monstrous. Lashed-twig spires jutted from aimless pebble-and-mud parapets, capped with toothy bark-shingled roofs. Pinecone stairways wound through forests of moss, into tree root caves reclaimed by hairy funnel-web spiders. Primitive lean-tos sheltered greedy stick golems with hoards of crusty pennies. It was not enchanting, not tranquil. It was a thing spawned from nightmare.

I wandered from one structure to the next. I did not blink; I was in a trance. Each house left me more unsettled than the one before. The spirals of desiccated beans looked cunning and ritualistic. The dank caves, infested and rank. Every tiny twig door opened to another moldering chamber in my divaricated brain — half of them hollow, the rest a shelter for overripe vitriol. My arm throbbed where the fly had bitten me; I scratched it until blood wormed down my arm.

Someone was following me. I couldn't say how long they'd been at it, but I knew if I turned I'd see them thirty feet back, between the peeling birch arms that sheltered the last fairy house grotesquerie.

I didn't dare turn.

Instead, I walked slowly onward. From behind me came the husky crack of a branch. The crunch of dried leaves. A slow, ragged breath. I fought the urge to look back: the terror of knowing outweighed even the fear of being followed. The air grew damp, thick. My chest ached from the effort of breathing, as if spiders had woven their funnel webs in the cavities of my lungs. I grew lightheaded, tripped on a root, put my boot through the roof of a fairy chapel. Vengeful wails rose from the forest floor. I glanced back, accidentally. I saw—

Can I even trust these eyes?

I ran. Thorns tore at my calves. I'd lost the trail. I clawed through underbrush, through sticky webs riddled with entombed flies, through chamber after chamber of fibrous gray matter. I was falling, I was screaming.

And then, abruptly, I was through. Into the broad, grasshopper-laden field opposite the hotel. I planted my palms on my knees, sucked down huge breaths of air. I tried to remember why I'd been running, what I'd seen when I looked back. But the memory had already begun to fray.

When I got to the room, Sumaira looked me up and down. "What *happened?*"

I told her I fell into some brambles. She wasn't convinced.

"Do you need to lie down?" Her body language belied her concern. Distracted, she walked to the window, looked outside. "Take a nap?"

"I'm fine, really." In truth, I was rattled. But not about the woods. "How was the lighthouse?"

"Huh? Oh, good. I ran into that guy again."

"Alex."

"Um, I think. You'd like him."

My nails dug into the meat of my palms. "I thought he was leaving."

"Yeah." She was still looking out the window. Searching. "Mechanic no-showed. He called the shop, and they said *he* canceled. By then they were booked through tomorrow."

"Convenient."

She didn't catch my meaning. She said, "You think Mr. Almandine interfered? To get him to pay for another few nights?"

"That's ridiculous."

She frowned at me. Finally, she came away from the window. "You sure you're okay?"

I had to tell her. Couldn't tell her. *Did you know a human can survive with half a brain?* "I'm being followed."

"What?" She didn't seem concerned. If anything, she looked incredulous. "Are you sure? We're in the middle of nowhere. Nobody even knows we're here." She looked me up and down again, clinically. "Sure you don't want to lie down?"

I looked out the window. Way out at sea, storm clouds knotted. "I'm sure."

-Ander

∽

ALEX,

I saw you with her this morning, from the third-floor lounge that overlooks the bay. Not that either of you were trying to hide. You sat on an old wooden bench, the kind with a brass plaque hammered to the front naming some rich Yankee donor. You tossed a wrench into the air, caught it, tossed it again. Sumaira stood nearby, laughing. She didn't look distracted, now. She looked exultant.

I know what you're doing.

When Sumaira came back to the room, there was grease on her hand. Motor oil, maybe. I'd been reading a book I found in the lounge. It was about the fairy houses. Staring at the pictures made my fingers go numb. I had to force myself not to look away.

I put the book down. "So. Have you psychoanalyzed him yet?"

It was a shitty thing to say. But the way she looked at you, I knew she saw a project. She used to look at me the same way.

The muscles on her face went stiff. "It's called *talking*, Ander. People do it sometimes."

I picked at the scab on my arm.

She let out a perfunctory sigh. "I think you'd like him."

"So I've heard."

"He reminds me of you, in a way. Except..."

Except, the old me.

She hesitated. "That bite doesn't look great. Think you should get it checked out?"

"By who? Mr. Almandine?"

"Stop it, Ander. I'm just concerned."

My gaze slid to the book in my lap. "About me."

"Ever since we got here, you've been...I don't know."

I almost told her. About how we didn't survive the accident that killed Mom and Dad with scrapes and bruises like I'd always said. How the door panel carved a trench through the crown of our skull, and the only way to save us — save *you* — was to rip out half our brain. And how the hospital agreed to foot the bill, for their precious research, under one condition: they'd transplant the orphaned hemisphere into the body of a brain-dead but otherwise healthy seventeen-year-old man. Boy.

I almost said, *I know Alex, because he used to be me.*

Instead, I said, "Maybe I'm not the one with the problem."

Sumaira almost hid her flinch. She looked at me, warily, like she would a wounded dog. "Let's get out of here. We could be in Boston by dinner. We can drop Ripley off. I'll buy you sushi. And in the morning..."

In the morning, she'd call my therapist.

You put these thoughts in her head. I can see your endgame.

I was at the window. Offshore, the storm was bearing down hard. Things would not improve here. Not with you around. Sumaira was giving me an out. I thought about going home. Leaving you behind, once and for all.

"No," I said. "I think we should stay."

-Ander

~

ALEX,

The storm made landfall this afternoon. Rain pummeled the shoreline. The wind uprooted a whole row of trees at the woods' edge. Hotel staff scrambled through the halls, shoving metal buckets under the worst of the leaks. Elsewhere, the wallpaper glistened and bulged. Ripley howled as the wind hammered the decrepit windows, slunk into the bathtub when the lightning struck. Sumaira crawled into the tub alongside him, held his trembling nose to her chest. The tide swelled, flooded the banks, overtook the bridge. A suspension line broke loose in the wind, writhed across both lanes.

Sometime after sundown, the rain slackened. The flags flapped fiercely, once, then hung limp. I opened a window. The woods were a wreckage, but the air smelled loamy and fresh. The sound of rain soothed me. The weight of you and me bled into the mud. Then Mr. Almandine knocked at the door.

He smiled, tight-lipped. "I regret to inform you that the bridge has sustained considerable damage and is presently impassable. Rest assured, we are amply provisioned until repairs are made. In the event of a medical emergency, there is a boat."

I hoped he didn't mean that old motorboat banging against the rocks by the tide pools. That thing would never make it across the bay.

Mr. Almandine moved on to the next room. I glanced down the hall. Past Mr. Almandine, someone stood at the end of the hall. I couldn't see their face around Mr. Almandine, but in their hand they held an intimidating wrench. A shiver passed through me. Mr. Almandine, who must've thought I was looking at him, turned. His face was stern, rigid, wholly unfriendly. I fled into our room. From the balcony, I peered around the corner to the mainland. A hundred porch lights glittered in the dark. So close. Unreachable.

"Convenient," I said.

Sumaira, who'd come up behind me, said, "Am I to blame for the weather now, too?"

I shook my head. "Not you."

-Ander

~

ALEX,

The power went out after dinner. We were in our room. Sumaira was reading some kind of legitimate literature. I was staring at the book on fairy houses. One house in particular had me ensnared. It was called *Old Alchemist*. It looked like the one I put my foot through the other day. The name got me thinking about an old history lecture — one of the few we hadn't slept through — of Enlightenment-age alchemists spawning homunculi from a horse's womb.

Then, abruptly, darkness overtook us.

"Shit," Sumaira said.

I checked my bag for a flashlight. No dice. "I'll go find some candles."

"It's alright." She was at the door suspiciously fast. "I'll go."

Her eyes were shiny black marbles against the sparse light of her phone.

"Okay," I said.

So she went.

And I followed. The hallway was darker even than our room. Voices carried from other rooms, like memories trapped in the discrete chambers of a hotel-sized brain. A child's cackle. The hushed laughter of a couple remembering what to do in the dark. A faint, airy wail. Underfoot, the staff scuttled about like wicked fairies.

Sumaira took the stairs. I followed, a flight behind. At the ground floor, she slipped across the shadow-drawn lobby to a room I didn't know existed — an old smoking room, studded with once lavish furniture.

That's where I found you.

You were sitting in a tired velvet armchair. She was standing very close, her bare knee brushing the worn wood leg of the chair. A soft yellow aura encased the two of you from the fat column candle in your left hand. On the table nearby: phone, keys, wrench.

I lingered at the doorway in a knot of shadow.

"...about to head out," you were saying in that casual way I do. I did. You do.

Sumaira glanced at the rain-streaked window. "Where to?"

"I wasn't expecting to stay so long. I'm running out of...things."

She looked at you in a way that made my teeth ache. "Meds?"

You nodded. Briefly, I worried: would you tell her which ones? Our medications are not common. Sumaira knows them by name.

"In this weather?" she said.

"The worst of it's passed."

"But the bridge—"

"It should be safe for foot traffic. There's a twenty-four-hour pharmacy on the other side."

Her eyes glistened. *Tell me more,* they said.

So you did. About the accident, the neural trauma, the seizures. The procedure that *took half your brain.* You didn't tell her what happened to that other half, though. The renegade half, the rotten half.

I looked at your scar, itched my arm, drew blood. I cursed under my breath, wiped the blood on my jeans. When I glanced up, Sumaira was right there. Holding the candle.

"The fuck are you doing?" Her eyes were slits, her lips thin. "Did you follow me?"

I craned past her. You were gone. The only evidence that you'd been there at all was the wrench, lying forgotten on the table.

"Where did he go?" I said.

"Did you follow me?"

I looked around, but it was too dark beyond the candle's radius. You could've been anywhere. "That man is dangerous."

"How do you know?" She did not sound worried. Just suspicious. "Do you know him?"

I didn't answer.

"Ander, what the fuck is going on with you?"

I looked at the wrench, at her, outside. She shoved the candle into my hands and stormed out into the rain. I rushed to the door. "It's still raining!"

Over her shoulder, she said, "The worst of it's passed."

I stood there, holding the door, watching her go. Even with the cloud cover at night, it was brighter outside than in the hotel. I could tell she was headed for the bridge. For you.

I blew out the candle and followed.

When I returned to the hotel, much later, I found Mr. Almandine lying in a pool of his own blood behind the concierge desk, beset by deer flies. Driven so far into the back of his skull that it was standing upright, was your wrench.

-Ander

~

DEAREST ALEX,

They said you're allowed to receive mail. I thought you should finally have these letters. I turned over copies to the police as well, in lieu of a verbal statement — though I doubt they'll give them more than a glance. They've amassed plenty of evidence. But you know all that.

Sumaira moved out. She said she hardly recognizes me anymore. And yet, it's like she's known you for years. She's going to wait for you. She seems to think this was all a big mistake, that some as-yet-unknown shred of evidence will come to light that will clear your name.

If only she knew.

The hospital phoned. They've seen the letters, too. Since your incarceration, the watchdogs have renewed their ethical concerns with our procedure. The field has improved dramatically these past years, rendering such techniques barbaric and unnecessary. They'd like to rescind their work. In turn, the Justice Department has agreed to commute your sentence through mental health diversion.

Rescind, Alex. They want to put us back together.

What fresh hell is this, I might ask, that they should stuff me into the skull of a killer? A man who would not settle for robbing me of body and soul. *Look*, they say, *the other half of this man, he is doing so well.* Because when have I ever been more than half a man? The *other* half. And now that they see how lost you are without me, they would vanish me, sweep under the rug this regrettable misstep. Make you whole again. You, not a villain, but a victim.

I don't have to go through with it, of course. They could make my life difficult, sure, but I am legally independent. I could say no.

But I don't think I'll do that.

See you inside.

Yours,
Ander

~

HEY BUD,

What joy it brings me to pen this, our happy ending.

It's raining again, hard, just like that night on Deer Fly Island. The view from your office — our office — *my* office — is superb. Looking down from the hillside onto all those houses in the gorge, they look just like those gnarled cityscapes in the woods. Like *Old Alchemist*, built by fairies, for dark purpose. Just like us.

Isn't that right, Alex?

When I look in the mirror — such a tall, stately mirror hanging from your wall — I am enamored. With a strong, steady hand I caress the soft stubble of our jaw. It's good to be home. I wonder: how much could you guess by the grin on my face as I entered the operating room? Did you know my plan? What I'd already done? Did it terrify you when I took your flaccid hand in mine? I saw how your body trembled, how the protests bubbled on your numbed lips, and died. It was almost sad. It was glorious.

Of course, by then it was too late. The pre-op was already inside you. Soon, I would be too. It didn't matter if you'd guessed how much I schemed from the moment I saw you across the dining room — or, perhaps, long before that. In truth, I suppose some part of me has been scheming from the time I woke up in another man's body, and looked over, and saw that you had won.

I was not going to let you win again.

I do feel bad for Mr. Almandine.

You should know that much of what I wrote was truth. I couldn't contradict Sumaira's testimony, after all. Can you blame me for taking some narrative liberties? I had to show them how unwell you were without me, how the thing they did to us was so very unfair. Everything I did on the island — sabotaging your spark plugs, phoning the mechanic to cancel your appointment — I did for us. And I *did* see you in the woods, you fucking ghoul, I swear—

Ahem. Water under the bridge.

Sumaira was right, a journal really can be therapeutic. It's not unlike our recent correspondence, really: mostly honest and pleasantly one-way.

~~Hheoooo~~

No, *one*-way. The doctors said there would be moments where the two hemispheres might struggle for control. I can feel you inside me even now, lurking in the inner chambers amongst your vile fairy horde. But lurk is all you'll do. I've always been the stronger half.

I've always been the killer.

Sumaira is calling from downstairs. I cooked her dinner. Vindaloo, her favorite. How she'll marvel that I guessed it! Not sure what to tell her about the dog. Such a tragedy, that he'd befall the same fate — a wrench from the same toolbox, even — as poor Mr. Almandine. But you know how that dog despised me. The growling would've made Sumaira suspicious, sooner or later.

Forever mine,
AlexAnderAlexAnderAlexAnderAlexAnderAlexAnderAlex...

Fragments (From a Film)

Avra Margariti

THE FIRST SHOT is a close-up of a hand splayed out on a dark-clothed table, luminously pale like a night-blooming cereus. We know the hand belongs to the director of the film, the one with the shaky but compelling camerawork.

Though the hand is rendered disembodied through the camera's framing, it's an inextricable part of a collective whole. The hand rotates once, twice, an elfin Houdini showing off its range of motion. Just when we're about to wonder what this hand would feel like pressed gently against our cheek, the hand slams itself against the table, again and again. We lean forward in our seats in the abandoned cinematheque, the director's sharp susurration of breath enfolding our eardrums.

There are twenty-seven bones in the human hand, and the director's are well and truly broken.

The hand, at last, is free to heal into its higher purpose.

But that is only the beginning.

THESE ARE the things we know for certain:
1) Bones grow back stronger after a fracture

2)   They grow back stranger, too

3)   One day we found a gilded cinema ticket tucked under our pillow or into our coat pocket or under a doormat, and we told no one

4)   We told no one at all

~

THE SECOND SCENE, we know through the limbic resonance spindling filament-networks between us, is cleverly shot through a mirror's reflection, ornately silver and angled just so to avoid revealing the camera and its handler.

The director is as genderless as they are faceless. This does not faze us, though we admit we each have our preferences. But to picture the director's face or identity is to commit a sacrilege, to break the compulsion of interconnectedness. Once, we might have compared the director to a stolen caryatid weary of museum-captivity, ruining their body so nobody else could. A fallen angel shattering the celestial corpus to escape its bonds. A snuff-film star making us, the viewers, complicit in their abuse.

We know much better than that now: Individualistic projections shrivel into atrophy inside the cinematheque.

In the mirror's reflection gapes the black hole of a belly button surrounded by unbroken expanses of flesh.

The knife glints like the mirror. Like our eyes, unblinking, as we watch.

The blade digs into the stomach cavity, disappearing into the deep-space interstices within. An upward motion unhinges the sternum, so that each organ can be tenderly removed, stored into a vat for later retrieval. Life-giving arteries tied off; nerves bundled like fresh poppies.

Organs are fragile things. They do not withstand damage well. Unlike bones, they are not here to be reborn.

The director grabs a mallet next, bends themself over a counter to reveal the naked crescent spine, the ribs — true, false, floating — the xylophone vertebrae. Their spine is ready to take the hammering. To grow back stronger, anew.

And we remember, as the director breaks their backbone, the

times when we failed to find ours. How we couldn't stand up to bosses or exes, how we cowered at a slur thrown at us in the street, how we couldn't pick up the phone and call our doctor or insurance company or lawyer's office, we didn't see our children or parents when scheduled because we couldn't stand to see the disappointment in their eyes.

One by one, the director breaks each rib and vertebra.

The camera, all-present, all-seeing, catches every fissure and crack.

WE EACH CAME to the cinematheque alone. Furtive, stealing glances at our stolen lives, the lives that had stolen our aspirations.

An automaton sat behind the ticket booth, humanoid from the waist up. We imagined their form arachnid under the old-wood desk, and we each admired this obsolete wonder of mechanics as we handed over our tickets. Although the automaton bore no eyes other than rusted cogs, it saw us, and saw in us the will to be rendered obsolete, too. Upgraded into something shiny and brand-new.

Thus, we were ushered past the rat-eaten velvet drapes, into the belly-dark of the chamber beyond. We know our way by heart now, the same touch-frayed ticket offering us admission, time after time.

We bear witness to the legs next, precious symbiotes of the skeleton.

The director sits in a wingback chair, the leather upholstery well-worn and well-loved. This, the love, puts us at ease. The camera is set on a tripod, the director's face cut-off but for their blissful-smiling lips. Our own lips respond in kind.

After all, this shattering has never been about causing the most damage. It is needful, but not merciless.

The director's mallet zeroes in on their fragile phalanges. Then: metatarsals, talus, fibula, tibia. Briefly, the pulverized flesh sloughs off.

We wonder if the slip of bone underneath is a familiar one, if we have seen it in X-rays or under bad cuts or burns, or even felt it with our fingers when we were self-hating enough to want to knead our flesh into non-existence. Then, the moment passes, because it doesn't matter whose bone this is. Soon, such solitary thoughts will never materialize again, in the fusing of our once-broken world.

Kneecap cracks echo. There are thirty bones in each leg. Some take more strength than others to break. We lean forward in our seats, a part of us lamenting how easier the process would be if we were there to help the director cleanly break the bone without sand-like particles and splinters. To hold their hands throughout, care for them afterward.

But we settle back in our seats, knowing that the process is part of the plan.

That for everyone to be connected — collective — they must first make a personal sacrifice.

We can't wait to understand one another, once all the world has faced the same uniting pain.

∼

THIS IS what we know about the film's director:

1) They are intimately familiar with pain; their own, but also the world's

2) The breaker of bones understands the world is a suppurating sore in need of a gentle-but-firm-handed debridement. They can tell when we've doom-scrolled for hours or cried ourselves to sleep or stood at the edge of a tall building and thought how easy it would be, how very easy...

3) The director knows the belief that pain makes us stronger is a false one, a dangerous thought to excuse the world's atrocities (the director is acquainted with those, too)

4) Pain is impossible to disengage from the needful things one must do to one's body

5) But the director loves us, all of us

6) And if it were up to them, they would never let any of us suffer any pain at all.

∼

WE HAVE BEEN HERE many times now. Briefly, we have joined the world beyond the cobwebbed cinematheque, past the yellowed marquee and the moth-eaten seats that cradle us like the cosmos. The world outside now feels like a fiction whose enforcement we have since outgrown. The people on the street are all separate and disconnected, like the unfused bones of an infant's skull. We want to tell them, *it won't always be like this, you'll see.* But we can't. Not yet.

Somewhere between finding the ticket and now, the desperate ennui that had guided our lives has broken and mended itself into a resolute sort of peace.

At last, the camera shows the director in full-frame. The vision of their skull deluges our eyes with Acheron tears. Their face is beloved, like we've seen it before in a dream — a balm between our waking nightmares.

We are still crying, still smiling, when the director swings their mallet on repeat, breaking every bone of their skull while blood and brains fly like vestigial pieces of that primordial dream.

THIS IS what we now know about ourselves:

1)   All our lives we've been adrift, bereft, and it took until finding this cinema ticket — like a blessed infestation of the mind — to realize it

2)   We are fragmented now, but not for long. There is comfort in that thought, caulking through the fractures

3)   And though we mourn our final departure from the abandoned cinematheque, there are filaments of interrelated purpose disseminating inside us

4)   The comfort lingers

SO WE LEAVE the cinematheque and go back home to garages and kitchens and garden sheds. We each pick the necessary implement — hammer, meat tenderizer, metal pipe — and stuff rags in our mouths in preparation for the clean break we've been craving.

There is no camera; there never was. We don't need one to be seen.

There are two-hundred-and-six bones in the human body.

We choose the hand first, always the hand, and feel our image travel across the atoms of air, into the minds of the new ticket-holders as they begin to awaken. The director has taught us better than to revel in pain, but we tolerate it well. Because it comes with the knowledge that we — the world's fragmented we — will heal stronger and stranger, too.

All the Devils Are Here

Mike O'Driscoll

He expected Harris any time now, had even ordered him a drink, the usual bourbon on the rocks. It sat on the counter, untouched and growing warm as the ice melted in the glass. The bar's patrons were mostly a self-consciously bohemian crowd, artists, musicians, writers, and the like. He felt at home in the *Pillar of Salt*, felt that he belonged, that he was among people who shared a similar view of the world. Non-judgemental, live and let live. He signalled for another beer but Jay, the insouciant young bartender, ignored him, turning instead to a dark-haired young woman he thought he recognised.

It was after seven and outside the light had begun to fade. He had been waiting almost an hour. In spite of the anticipation he'd felt when he arrived, he was becoming agitated. The young woman smiled at him and he felt her name on the tip of his tongue. Her red t-shirt had the words *This thing of Darkness* written across the front. He made to greet her but the words stalled in his mouth when he realised he didn't know her at all. He felt a little disoriented, just as he had that afternoon when he called into the corner Spar near his flat. Musa, who worked the checkout, nearly always made time for a quick chat while ringing up his items, but this afternoon he'd been a little off, barely saying a word. Perhaps Musa's boss had been on his case, he thought, ticking him off for wasting customers' time, but as he'd left the store, he'd caught sight of Musa laughing and joking with the next customer. He'd let the snub, if that was what it was, trouble him more than it should have.

It was Marcia, a former girlfriend, who had introduced him to Harris, though she had called him Jamie, a name he felt completely inappropriate for the tall, fair-haired young man who had immediately clasped his arms in a warm, friendly manner and said, "So you're the actor." Not a question, not spoken in that sceptical, even disbelieving tone he was used to hearing on first acquaintance, but a simple acknowledgement of fact, even if it was something of a stretch, and had been for some time, to call himself anything of the sort. The truth was he hadn't performed for going on three years. His last decent role had been in rep with a touring company, playing Bailey in an adaptation of *A Good Man is Hard to Find*. He had been up for the part of The Misfit, which he thought the more challenging role, but that went to another actor. There had been some bad feeling initially between the two men, but they had managed to put their differences behind them and it had seemed they would become friends, especially after a successful tour led to the production earning a six-week run at a small London theatre. The play had just opened when Covid struck and the country went into lockdown, putting paid to everything, including the nascent friendship.

But still, even though in the interim he had worked gigs in hospitality, retail support, dog walking, and, for the last four months, transcription — mostly of medical audio files, but occasionally for a podcast — he still thought of himself, first and foremost, as an actor. Harris, who, Marcia had informed him, was also in performing, had seemed to recognise his true vocation, and though he was flattered, he'd been honest enough to admit it had been a while. Harris had enquired about his present employment and on hearing of his ongoing contribution to the gig economy, had suggested he make changes to his life. He'd been taken aback when Harris had said, "It pains me to see someone of your abilities wasting yourself on such things. You need to show the world who you really are."

Not having acted for so long, it was difficult to remember the specific nature and quality of these abilities. He supposed he moved well on stage or in front of a camera; his voice was good, naturalistic in tone, and he had mastered a wide range of accents; and some people said he had charisma, though he was too modest to say so himself. He worked hard and learned fast. These were, he imagined, precisely the sort of abilities to which Harris referred, but when he sought confirmation, though Harris acknowledged their importance, he spoke, somewhat obliquely, of "other things."

At last he caught Jay's eye and he came and picked up the glass of warm bourbon and held it in front of his face, swirling it as he scrutinised the liquor, sporting a tattoo of some oddly geometric symbol on his forearm. "What's wrong with it?"

"Nothing's wrong with it. It's for my friend."

Jay made a show of looking around, as though searching for this friend. "You want another one?"

"Another beer."

Jay slipped away, taking the glass of bourbon.

A deep resentment stirred inside him. "Bring me another one of those," he called out. If Jay heard, he gave no sign. Dick, he thought. The last time he'd been here, with Harris, the young bartender had been all over them like a fly on shit. Couldn't do enough for them. Harris had picked up on it and had complimented Jay on his attentiveness. Hard to tell if he was being sarcastic, but it had seemed that way. Harris had the power to make people pay attention to him, even to fawn over him. It was almost sickening to watch. Maybe it was one of those mysterious attributes he'd spoken of, the ones possessed by all good performers.

He checked his phone but there were no missed calls, no messages. It was gone seven-thirty and his agitation was blooming toward exasperation. The bar was half-full, mostly familiar faces from the neighbourhood. He glimpsed a pale, slender hand resting on the counter nearby. Jay brought a pint of Peroni and slapped it down in front of him. No bourbon. When he mentioned it, Jay said, "I thought you didn't like it."

He said, "I never said that."

"You want a fresh one?"

"What did I just say?"

Jay looked aggrieved. "Do you want it or not?"

He was tempted to give him a piece of his mind, but something in the wall mirror behind Jay disturbed him. He had expected to see a woman on the stool just along the counter, but nobody sat there, and when he looked down, there was no hand. Looking back at the mirror, he saw a man in blue approaching and quickly said yes, before turning to greet Harris.

"Jim," he said to the man he saw wasn't Harris at all, but someone else, a bearded man called Foley, somebody he sometimes spoke to, shared a drink and a joke with.

"What?" said the man.

"My mistake," he said. "I didn't recognise you — thought you were someone else."

"Someone else?"

"Yes, sorry."

"Who?"

"You wouldn't know him."

"How do you know?"

"He's not been here often. I'm sure you haven't met him."

"What's his name?"

"Harris. Jim Harris."

"You mean James?"

"You know him?"

"Course I do. Everybody here knows James."

He was surprised. On the few occasions he and Harris had been to the *Pillar of Salt* together, they'd hardly spoken to anyone else, apart from Marcia, who had turned up one night about six weeks back with Harris in tow. The way they had acted around one another, it was clear they were in a relationship, though he had only seen them together that one time. It didn't bother him since his own relationship with her had lasted barely three months and they had remained good friends. Thinking about it now, he realised he hadn't seen Marcia since that night. "Well," he said, "my apologies, Foley, for confusing the two of you."

Foley's questioning look unsettled him. Feeling the need to offer clarity, he said, "I don't mean you look like him, so much as I saw your jacket in the mirror. He always wears blue."

Foley looked incredulous. "What exactly are you saying?"

His unease grew like a late afternoon shadow. Jay brought the fresh bourbon.

"Get this fella," Foley said to Jay, who laughed and shook his head.

"I'd rather not," Jay said.

"Says I shouldn't wear blue."

"That's not what I said," he tried to explain, wishing Harris were there to clear the matter up. He had a talent for concision, for using precisely the right words, and only those words, to make himself understood. Nothing superfluous about him. Probably came with being a performer. "What I meant was, when I saw Foley in the mirror, I thought it was —"

"Who's Foley?" Jay said.

Foley, or perhaps not Foley at all, said, "No idea." He grinned at Jay who handed him the glass of bourbon. He took it and shuffled across the room to join a small group at a nearby table.

"That was my..." he began to say but caught himself, no longer sure whether he had ordered the drink. Probably better to wait until Harris arrived. Who wanted to drink a warm bourbon anyway? He sipped the beer and glanced at the spot on the counter where the hand had rested, wondering who it had belonged to. The long fingers suggested a woman's hand, but it might have been a man's. Except, he remembered, the nails had been painted red. Odd that he hadn't seen her face.

It had been a funny sort of day. The morning had been spent transcribing what had initially seemed a mundane medical treatise on the psychopathology of Cotard's Syndrome. He'd listened as the warm, familiar voice explained how, in phenomenological terms, in more than 100 case studies, the most frequently found symptoms were nihilistic delusions concerning the body and existence. Yet, in the process of transcribing the study, he began to feel a singular sense of disconnection that, although he could hear what was said on the audio file, left him with little sense of its precise meaning, or even the general gist of the subject under discussion. In effect, for a time, it was as though the voice was speaking in tongues, and when, after some minutes had passed, he glanced at the screen, what he saw was an unpunctuated slew of unfamiliar, yet vaguely onomatopoeic words. It was only when he paused the file and attempted to speak the glossolalia that he came to himself and realised his mind had wandered.

He scrolled back through the last four pages he had typed, dismayed to find they were gibberish. Unable to account for it, he'd replayed the file and started over, managing to get through the rest of the paper without mishap.

He had eaten lunch at a sushi bar on the high street a quarter mile from the flat. It helped clear his mind to get out and take the short walk through the park. When he had finished his shrimp tempura roll and was on his way back to the flat, Harris had called wanting to know if he'd made progress with the series of mental exercises he had given him. They were meant to boost confidence and sharpen one's critical faculties. "In essence," Harris had explained, "they'll help you get your mojo back."

He had, in truth, been somewhat irritated at the suggestion that he was lacking in confidence, and that his critical faculties weren't up to muster, but he understood that Harris had his best interests at heart and if, even mistakenly, his friend perceived that such exercises would help get his acting career back on track, then it seemed churlish not to at least attempt one or two.

When he told Harris he'd been practicing the exercises twice a day for the last five days but was, as yet, unable to identify any increase in self-esteem, or indeed detect signs of his allegedly misplaced mojo, his friend assured him only good things were coming. He had only to stick to the plan, and sooner rather than later, things would be different for him. They'd arranged to meet in the *Pillar of Salt* that evening, when, Harris told him, he had something to reveal, something that would show the extent to which his life was about to change.

In the afternoon he had transcribed an episode of a somewhat sensationalist true crime podcast with vaguely supernatural undertones. On the whole, the content was lurid, but the show's creator and host had worked in television, once upon a time, acted in numerous crime dramas and soaps, and was still well-regarded in the industry. It had been Harris who had tipped him off about the gig. The man knew people, he had heard, producers and casting directors, and if he were to take the job, Harris suggested, who knew what opportunities might be forthcoming. The episode he had worked on appeared, at first, little different to the two previous episodes he had transcribed. The presenter had a predilection for cases that involved the slaying of beautiful women by jealous, frequently drug-crazed, lovers, or mysterious psychopaths with a penchant for brutal, ritualist killings, the sort of tales he imagined had little to do with reality or truth, and that had once filled the pages of pulp paperbacks with screaming, semi-naked women on the covers.

Nevertheless, he had worked diligently, endeavouring to add polish to the gruesome narration in the hope of impressing the podcast's host. The story concerned the disappearance of a young female actor and the subsequent discovery of her horribly mutilated body. Framed for her murder, the plot had focused on her lover's quest to discover the truth and thus prove his innocence. Though it all seemed hackneyed and distasteful, he had found himself disturbed by some aspects of the tale, elements that provoked in him an odious sense of familiarity, even of intimacy, such that he had been able to predict some of the gruesome events before they were revealed. The extent to which he had allowed himself to be caught up in the story came as a shock, one that had left a bad taste in his mouth that even now, midway through his second beer, still lingered.

When Jay drifted once more into his orbit, he caught his attention and ordered another Peroni and, thinking Harris's arrival must now be imminent, a large Jim Beam. He slugged back what remained of his second beer and caught sight of the man he had mistook for Foley sitting with a group of people in a corner booth. Surely, he thought, the blonde woman was Esther, a dancer, and the tall woman with glasses and stern mouth was her friend Sarah or Sally, something like that. Two of the men in the group of six or seven, were musicians or artists Marcia had introduced him to when they were going out. And of course Foley had been part of that set — that's how they knew each other — and thinking this, he looked closely at the man he'd thought was Foley, studying the face, the carefully trimmed circle beard, the dark, slicked back hair, and the way his mouth curled when he laughed, which it did now as he listened to something Sarah, or Sally, said.

It *is* Foley, he thought, feeling slightly disoriented, a sensation amplified moments later when the man — Foley — looked at him and winked, before turning back to the group and carrying on his conversation.

What did it mean? What the hell was he playing at? It occurred to him that he was the subject of some cruel joke. Why? What had he done to any of them? He turned away, feeling a slight sense of mortification. You're overreacting, he told himself. They're your friends. Go and join them, show them you can take a joke. He slid off the bar stool and took a step toward them but stopped abruptly, realising that nobody in the group was who he had thought they were. Not his friends at all, but more people he didn't know. Rattled, he returned to the stool, picked up the Jim Beam and drank half the glass. Where in Hell was Harris? Why hadn't he called? It made no sense.

He took out his phone and called his friend. After a few seconds, the voicemail service cut in and instructed him to leave a message. "Hey Jim," he said. "It's me. Just wondering where you're at. It's —" he checked the time and blinked, taken aback, "— eight thirty. I've been here like, since well before seven." He paused, not wanting to appear anxious, but was unable to entirely shake off the feeling of disquiet. "No worries if you're running late. Just give me a call back and I'll have a large Jim Beam waiting."

He finished the bourbon and chased it with a slug of Peroni. The bar was busier now, and bodies crowded around him. His eyes felt gritty and began to water and the bar reeked of smoke as if half the clientele had lit up, but when he scanned the room he saw that wasn't so. An old tune ran through his head, some easy listening thing about hearts on fire. He tried to shake it off and catch the bartender's attention. Not Jay, but some other guy, someone who might have been Jay's older brother. He sniffed the air and said, "You get that?"

"Get what?" said the marginally older bartender.

He coughed, and gestured at the air, feeling small particles on his tongue. "That."

When the man shrugged, he pointed at the two empty glasses and asked for the same again.

It was inconsiderate of Harris, he decided. He could at least have called to let him know he was running late. Had it not been for this mysterious — but in all reality, he felt, probably banal — revelation Harris had promised, he would have left already. He was tempted, momentarily, but decided instead to wait until he'd finished the drink he'd just ordered. He stood and pushed his way through the jostling crowd to the toilet. One or two people called his name but it was hard to tell if they meant him or someone else, or perhaps they spoke in jest.

It was much quieter when he returned. A pint of lager stood on the counter next to a fresh bourbon on the rocks. He wondered what it was that Harris wanted to tell him. For the first time since they'd met, he felt maybe his friend had a tendency toward the melodramatic. How could Harris possibly know that his life was about to change? In what way? Feeling a little deflated, he attempted to lift his mood by engaging with one of Harris's exercises. He closed his eyes and, beginning with the soles of his feet, he noticed the sensations there, any coldness or warmth, if there was a tingling in his toes. Slowly, his focus drifted upward, scanning the lower part of his legs, trying to avoid thinking about what he felt, only to observe. His attention moved up past his groin to his stomach, where he was struck by the absence of sound, those internal squeaks and groans whose presence signalled life. Maybe it's a good thing, he thought, showing he was focused. But to hear nothing at all? To drown in an ocean of silence? Opening his eyes, he saw people drinking and talking, a scene of normality, until he realised he could hear nothing, not at first, not until two or three seconds had passed and then it seemed as if he were watching a badly dubbed foreign move, where the actors words played catch-up with their mouths.

A blue swathe cut through the crowd, was lost momentarily only to reappear among a group of people clustered around a table. Harris? He raised his arm and waved, shouting Harris's name.

"Are you all right, dear?" a brazen woman asked.

"Marcia?" he said.

"It's not him," she said.

"No," said her familiar.

"My apologies," said the woman. "We thought you were someone else."

He turned away and looked again for anybody dressed in blue. He was sure it had been Harris; the man had been searching for someone, for him. Dammit, why didn't Harris just call him? Instead, he grabbed his phone and saw a notification, a WhatsApp message from Jim. *Are you there yet?* the text said. What does he mean, am I there yet? Where does he think I am?

Jay stood in front of him, smiling. "Good news, then?" His

hands lay on the counter, unpainted and not smooth at all. He nodded at the phone.

"I've no idea," he said, flustered and uncertain. What had happened to the other bartender, the one who resembled an older version of Jay? He forced himself into another of Harris's exercises, a process of cognitive restructuring that Harris had assured him would help counter negative thoughts. He thought about the last audition he had attended, and how he had failed to get the part. It was because he had been hopeless. No — you just haven't heard back from them yet. They'll tell you when they've made up their minds. If you didn't get the part, they'll tell you why and you can learn from that. Okay, that's much more positive. *It's a lie.* Why did you mess up that transcript today? You didn't mess up, you were simply distracted for a couple of moments. It could happen to anyone. *It happened to you.* I was tired and my mind was focused on other things. *Your mind is slipping.* Harris isn't coming. Not true, he's my friend, he has things to tell me. *He's laughing at you, right now.* We're friends. *He sees right through you, all the way to the emptiness.*

A cold, ghastly feeling welled up inside and he whimpered like a frightened dog. He picked up the bourbon, took a swig and felt something soft and gelatinous brush against his lips, his tongue. He spat the alcohol back into the glass where two orbs bobbed up and down in the amber liquid, watching him with an avid desire. A flash of blue reflected off the surface of the glass. He spun round, searching for Harris among the listless, yammering bodies, thinking, he could be here, he could be any one of them. It occurred to him that he ought to respond to Harris's message, to let him know that he was here, that he had been here all along. A disturbing notion came to mind: what if Harris had already been and gone? What if, upon arrival, he had searched the bar — it had been busier a while ago — and, having failed to locate him, had left?

He reached for his phone but it was no longer in his jacket pocket. It lay on the counter next to the empty bourbon glass, a picture on the screen of two eyes floating in a glass. He knew it couldn't possibly be real. The glass was empty and he had only imagined the pair of glutinous spheres drowning in the liquor.

"Nice one," said Jay, indicating the phone. His tattoo was different somehow, as if the object it depicted had melted.

"You saw it?" he said.

"I'm not blind." Jay's eyes fogged with smoke. "You should be on stage."

"What do you mean?"

"You know what I mean."

"He's a magician," said the girl with the dark hair, the one he'd thought he recognised. "A conjuror."

"He makes people disappear."

"I see it all with my eyes of pearl," said the girl, laughing.

He picked up the phone, doing his best to ignore them and clumsily typed a brief text to Harris.

"See how he feigns maladroitness."

"It's all ignis fatuus with him," said Jay.

I'm here, he wrote. *I've been here all night. Please come.*

The lights had dimmed a little, and there was that song again, but sung differently this time, in an unfamiliar language, but definitely the same tune. What was it Harris had said about a man of his abilities? Where were they now? What even were these abilities Harris had seen in him? He didn't feel himself, and it was no help at all to see the dark-haired girl slough off her skin and step from it as if casting off a dress she had tried on but decided against. No solace in seeing other patrons begin to peel the flesh from their faces, exposing the nightmares that lurked beneath. He gripped the counter's edge to steady himself.

He fumbled for the phone when it rang, and saw Harris's face on screen, caught in a smile, with a blue light in his eyes. He pressed the answer button. "Harris?"

"Yes?" said Harris.

"Where are you?"

"I'm here."

"I've been waiting all night."

"I'm here now."

"You're where?"

The stench of smoke returned, and left an acrid taste in his mouth. His voice sounded like gravel when he tried to speak but he felt compelled to make himself understood. "What was it — the thing you were going to tell me?"

"You've noticed then?"

"Noticed what?"

"That things are changing," said Harris. "Like I said they would."

Something hot and cloying in the air, in the way it settled about him. He said, "You never said it would be like this."

"No, I didn't."

"I think I'm in Hell," he heard himself say.

"You can't be." Harris's voice was close. "Because Hell is empty, and …" His words were lost beneath the slow, heavy thud of heavy, beating wings.

Fliers

Gordon Brown

YOU REMEMBER IT, don't you?

The first that arrived.

It waited for you on the carpet, slipped under a crack in the door. You almost stepped on it in your hurry. You barely spared it a look. Not the first one. You left it sitting there with the take-out menus and oil change coupons and the property manager's notice about early lease renewal.

It was waiting for you when you got back.

Black. Glossy. Barely larger than an index card. And you might have thrown it away with the rest of the junk mail if it hadn't felt strangely heavy in your hands. If it hadn't felt oddly slick beneath your fingers. If there wasn't something about it you couldn't quite ignore.

You remember what it said the first time.

HOW YOU CAN KNOW YOU'RE GOING TO HEAVEN

That's all it was.

Another little religious tract. Some mass-mailed flier with a portrait of a smiling, dough-faced pastor on the back and John 3:16 and the address of the church that sent it.

But there wasn't any of that when you turned it over.

No familiar verse, no sympathetic face.

Flat darkness. Nothing else.

And you flipped it back again, didn't you? Because you hadn't gotten it right. You read it carefully this time and the sharp white font on the glossy paper read:

HOW CAN YOU KNOW YOU'RE GOING TO HEAVEN?

Which was the same thing.

Wasn't it?

You dropped the glossy black card in the trash with the rest of the junk mail. You didn't think about it the rest of the night and slept a deep and dreamless sleep.

You remember the last time you slept without dreaming. Maybe you don't.

There was another card in the morning.

WHAT HAPPENS WHEN YOU'RE UNCONSCIOUS

The question mark was missing from this one. Conspicuously absent. The space where it should have been seemed darker than the rest of the card. You brought the paper to your eye. Now that you looked, the rest of the card seemed darker than the space that should've carried the question mark. Or was it the other way around? You looked closer still. You almost had it.

The angry buzz in your pocket made you jump. It was your cell phone. Work wanted to know where you were. You looked at the clock and realized just how long you'd been standing there. You sprinted out the door, tossing the flier in the dumpster outside.

You're not sure why, but before you threw it, you tore it up.

There should have been white fibers where the cardstock ripped and peeled. Inside was just as black.

You tried typing the words into your computer at your job. You found articles about anesthesiology and the science of sleep. You entered what you remembered from the day before. You got links to religious sites. Videos of men sweating and shrieking behind pulpits. But the words didn't fit like they should have, did they? There was something different — something terribly different —

between what you saw on the screen and what was stamped on the cards.

You just couldn't figure out *what*.

There was one waiting for you when you got home.

And wasn't that a nasty surprise?

A little square, just slipped into the hallway, so perfectly dark you thought at first a hole had opened in the floor.

You meant to throw it away without reading it. You told yourself — promised yourself — if you ever got another…

But you couldn't help yourself, could you?

DO NOT COMPLY

It never said with what.

You picked it up, feeling that same disquieting weight. The almost-wet texture of the gloss. The smell of it. Soft. Cloying.

You tucked the flier gingerly in your pocket. You didn't like the idea of it so close to you, so you removed it again and carried it outside. The door opened across the walkway. That neighbor you never spoke to emerged from the opposing darkness, holding the same card and looking just as uneasy as you. Neither of you said anything. You tiptoed down to the leasing office and filed separate complaints, gripping the pen tightly over the forms. Unsure of what to write. How to explain it.

You tried "threatening messages," but that looked idiotic. You crossed it out, making tight, violent loops to obliterate the chance of anyone reading it. You tried "junk mail" and "prank." Those didn't fit either. You crossed both out and stopped suddenly as your neighbor hurried away from the manager's desk. He didn't look at you as he passed. You couldn't help but wonder why.

Of course, it might've been him. Easiest thing in the world.

He could've watched for when you left in the morning. Could've watched for when you came back. Could've grabbed himself a copy of those repulsive little notes and stepped out of his door at just the same moment, making certain you saw, making it look for all the world like he was getting them too.

But you couldn't figure out why.

You lay on your bed, traveling the empty miles between night and morning as the question asked itself. Why does anyone do anything? Who knows what people get up to when their doors are locked and the blinds are drawn? Tuck a thousand people away in their thousand little boxes and some will start to *rot*, and rot will want to *spread*. There's only one way to be normal. There are countless ways to be crazy.

There was another flier in the morning.

HOW CAN YOU KNOW YOU'RE GOING TO HEAV

The words were crisp but the alignment was off. The question — if it *was* a question — fell off the edge of the sheet. You made another complaint at the leasing office. There was a line when you got there. Everyone carrying the same black card. The property manager shuffled out to apologize. She promised everyone the courtesy patrol would be vigilant. She tried to keep an even tone but you saw dark crescents under her eyes. You wondered if she'd been getting them too.

Someone in the crowd whispered what no one wanted to say out loud.

"It's getting worse."

Someone else said: "Accelerating."

You stayed awake that night.

You never thought about it before, did you? How easy it would be for someone to tiptoe quietly up the stairs in the dark, dead hours. How they could be right outside your window, face against the glass. Or wiggling just *anything* through the cracks in your doorframe.

Easiest thing in the world.

So, you pulled up a chair. Forced yourself to lean against the door with your eye at the peephole. For a terrible second, a gut-twisting second, you wondered if someone might already be out there. Staring back. Leering. Some shifting, distorted face.

There was nothing.

Nothing at all.

You commanded yourself to feel relieved. Deep down you knew it meant that they hadn't arrived yet.

So you waited.

You and everyone else.

A hundred eyes at a hundred peepholes, sweeping back and

forth over their little illuminated islands of pavement. A hundred sets of ears straining against the silence as the hours slipped by, as the distant rattle of trucks and cars grew fewer and farther between, until the world fell away entirely.

The sun rose in the morning. It cracked and bled out across the sky and you realized you'd been sleeping. You looked down at the entrance-way floor.

It was empty and clean.

Unkempt and exhausted, but still feeling triumphant. You brushed your hair and splashed water on your face. You headed outside with a grin.

It faded when you saw what waited for you on your car.

WHAT HAPPENS WHEN YOU'RE UNCONSCIOUS
WHAT HAPPENS WHEN YOU'RE UNCONSCIOUS
WHAT HAPPENS WHEN YOU'RE UNCONSCIOUS

The letters smeared together — the usual definition now blurred and angry. You looked up and down the street. Every car had them. Some on the windshield. Some behind.

You tried telling yourself it was an elaborate joke. A social experiment. The thought of it intruded on you at work — kept rising out of your mind like black, wriggling things out of a backed-up drain. Rationalizing it made it worse. Like picking at a scab. Like digging around in the soft, raw skin underneath.

The idea of someone — no, not that. The *picture*. The *image* of someone sitting in the dark, bent low over a screen, pouring years of sickness and malice out onto page after page after page.

Infecting them.

There was no getting rid of *that* thought once it squirmed across your mind. It kept coming back. The cards might be diseased things. Contagious things. Modern-day smallpox blankets, delivered by someone hoping you'd catch whatever mental leprosy they had.

Unless it wasn't mental.

You jumped when you realized that, didn't you?

Because who could say there wasn't something other than gloss coating those little postcards? You remembered the anthrax scares. The urban legends about lipstick messages scrawled on motel mirrors reading "Welcome to the AIDS club." And what about those pictures in your head? Unbidden visions of a long, lurid, scab-covered tongue rolling lovingly over the surface of the paper. A trail of mucous coating and caking and drying like varnish. Softening when you picked the flier up. Sweating and seeping through the soft skin of your fingers.

Easiest thing in the world.

And then it was tougher to imagine any resentful, greasy, would-be school shooter having the patience for all this. Tougher to entertain the notion of any Bible-thumping abortion bomber being so methodical. The idea of a quiet, stuttering groundskeeper with corpses in his crawlspace sounded like something out of a cartoon.

One by one, you crossed out the suspects. No new ones took their place. There was only a big, laughing *empty* where a person ought to be.

You started leaving work early. For the briefest time, you thought you might finally catch it if you could surprise it. You're not sure when you started blaming an *"it"* instead of a *"him"* or *"her"* or *"them."*

It fit better.

Of course, you never did catch anything. The fliers were always waiting. Always a little more distorted than before. Always a little more wrong.

Soon enough they'd be unreadable. Soon enough there'd be nothing waiting but a plain, black card.

You weren't going to be there when it happened.

You broke your lease early. The tired, hollow expression on the property manager's face told you that you hadn't been the first.

All through the weekend you stayed awake packing, pitching half of everything you owned just to make things faster. You hired movers. You turned in your keys. You found a new place, clear across town. It doubled your drive, but still…

But still…

But still, even now, you can't quite shake it, can you?

You've got this pit down inside you can't dig out of. You're still worried. Still waiting. Still slowing the car to a crawl as you come home in the evening. You're opening the door slowly — letting the light spread inside, inch by inch.

It's perfectly empty. Nothing there.

Nothing yet.

Rippling Salt, Like Rolling Waves

Jorja Osha

THESE DAYS I hardly sleep so when the call comes in and they tell me that they've found Lola's body down in the salt pit my bleary mind can only selfishly think *'at least it's not her.'* It's only when I'm already on the road does my brain actually kick into gear and I try to figure out how she even got there, some thirty miles out and without a car. But that's exactly where she is by the time I duck under the tape, partially buried beneath a sea of pink crystals face down and dressed only in her underwear.

Luckily we're so far off from the town that there's no need for crowd control. The only ones not carrying a set of credentials for one thing or another are the Walcrests. They're the ones who found Lola just as the sun began to crack the horizon. Cortland tells me he doesn't think they're involved — as if any of us had given thought to the possibility — but he's new and doesn't know any better as of yet.

The Walcrests are a fisher couple, have been for the last eight years. I don't have to ask what they were doing in the vicinity, there's no need. You could set the clock by just watching them, always running on routine. A glance to my watch tells me that they were just on their way down to throw out their nets for the day. From where their house is they have no choice but to pass the pit to get down to the beach.

Lola on the other hand, she had no business being down this way. Ever. Not when she couldn't swim. Not when she was as much a native as myself and knew that there were just some things you needed to give a wide berth to.

For a moment I try to remember Lola's face but the longer I stare down at the back of tangled hair the harder it becomes as footsteps approach me from behind.

"They're going to go down soon," Reyes says though I barely catch the words over a whistling gale that comes out of nowhere.

That's when I smell it. It's not the usual smell of salt and water or even rotting fish that gets carried on the wind when you're this close to the sea. This is sweet, cloyingly. Like coolant leaking in a bakery and it's heavy on my tongue. Another reminder of how much I hate being out here. Another reminder that the only reason I keep answering these calls like a desperate lover hoping for a reconciliation that will never come is because I'm hoping *she'll* be one of the bodies that finally get called in. Of course there's another reason I might get a call but that one jostles the half-eaten breakfast sandwich and iced chai in the pit of my stomach to such a degree that it nearly reverses its natural course through my body.

I must look as sick as I feel because Reyes puts an arm around my shoulder and draws me up against him. His aftershave and cigarette smoke just barely overpowers the burning sweet scent that's started to fill my nostrils. But there's something else too, wafting about in the air, and it's coming off of him. *Meat*. Raw and bloody.

"You smell it too?" he asks when another breeze sends the sweet odor sweeping over us.

Everyone else is too busy tugging on hazmat suits, canvassing the area or questioning the Walcrests to pay any attention to us but I still remain silent, offering a quick nod before I shake out of his grasp. It's not tight, never is, but I feel like prey around the man in situations like this.

Steadying myself, I walk closer towards the lip of the pit. The drop is steep enough to keep me from getting too close. I have no intention of joining Lola.

This close the scent is sharper, brighter, but I've grown accustomed to it even though it still makes my eyes water the way no onion ever could. Pushing my glasses up I blink a couple of times then wipe my jacket sleeve across my face to finally focus on where Lola is partially buried.

That's when I see it.

Rippling salt like rolling waves. It would be easy for anyone to mistake it for simple wind disturbance but I know better. Reyes knows too, yet he grabs my arm when I open my mouth to tell the two men along with Cortland to back off.

"We need the body."

The way he says '*we*' gives me the sensation of teeth grazing against my neck. Hot, humid breath against the side of my face counters the chilly gust hitting me from the other side. Once more I nod. I know he's right but that doesn't mean I like it. Leaving Lola down there would be a mistake though and we didn't have time for any more of those.

"Cortland," I call to the man and watch him run to meet me looking a little too eager.

His face is red and windburned. He's clearly not used to the climate. I also doubt he knows what he's actually signed up for but he finds out soon enough when I reach inside my jacket and pull out the firearm I keep habitually tucked in my holster. Cortland looks startled as I open the cylinder of the worn revolver and push a single red painted bullet into one of the open chambers. Reyes, when I glance over to him, is staring down at the waves of pink salt. They've gotten larger now, those waves. And when I look back at Reyes I catch the manic look in his eyes that he doesn't even try to hide. That's when I remember the gun in my hand.

"Boric acid is relatively safe," I say to Cortland as I aim down towards one of the waves. "Borax however, that's corrosive to the eyes."

Cortland looks confused but that's only because he doesn't see it. I do though and that's all that matters. Just barely hidden beneath the sea of salt a smattering of eyes blink open peering directly up at us.

I fire and hear a wet popping sound that snaps through the air around us like one thunderous clap of hands.

And like racers on the line the two men in their red hazmat suits take the plunge as the thing I've struck shrieks and lurches towards the far side of the pit where the tide barely laps at the perimeter. The closer it gets the more we can see of it.

The cloying scent that catches on the wind nearly suffocates me as I observe the horror below. I lurch, almost doubling over, but somehow keep down my breakfast unlike Cortland who trips over his feet in retreat, heaving and gagging noisily. I, on the other hand, inhale deeply watching the pink, slick thing with too many tails slither towards the sea. The bloody gash, once an eye now ruined by a well-aimed bullet, glares back at me from a malformed face, looking too much like my sister's, on the creature's back.

I turn and head to my car before I can start imagining it actually *is* her.

~

REYES IS as happy as a pig in mud when the coroner calls him down to the morgue. At least one of us can be happy, but I don't begrudge him these moments of what amounts to euphoria for him. He puts in more work than anyone realizes and, well, he needs to eat. Lola doesn't have anyone to claim her body anyways and even if she did we still wouldn't release her. Her respiratory system is a mess. Shiny white polyps and sticky, scaly webbing. It was pulsating when she was cut open, spilling out like crab boil on the metal slab and probably still was by the time Reyes got downstairs.

He smells like carrion when I see him again climbing into my front passenger seat. I pretend he's not there as I mix my salad. It's a pretense I can only keep up until he begins talking.

"That's the sixth one this month and not one of them has been your sister."

I must've not been expecting that, though I should have in retrospect. Either way I miss the carrot between my molars and instead bite into my tongue. Hard.

In the past I wouldn't have hesitated to put space between me and Reyes the minute I tasted copper spread across my taste buds, but we have long reached an understanding so I stay still and swallow.

"You said I could have the month. There's a week and a half left." I know I sound desperate but I don't have the energy to hide it. I'm running on three hours sleep thanks to a combination of night terrors and this morning's early call.

In response Reyes makes this noise in the back of his throat. It's a steady clicking like a thousand fingers thrumming along the length of hollow bones. I have yet to decipher what it means but there's one thing I'm certain of. It's a positive sign.

That night I dream of Lola dancing in the salt pit with her rotten insides fluttering in the breeze. She's not alone either. Behind her something lurches towards me until I'm able to see that ruinous eye staring at me with its angry red wound.

That sickeningly sweet scent greets me when I wake up drenched in sweat. When I look to my left I see that my bedroom window is open.

~

No one is surprised when next week arrives and Cortland's desk is cleared out. No one knows when it was exactly that he left but I can only hope that he left in the morning. It's a day later that I learn he didn't. It was the middle of the night.

I catch the dark shape of Reyes standing in the middle of the road facing away from me when I drive up, my headlights dim. It's only once I'm parked do I turn on the high beams where I can make out Cortland's car parked off to the side. The driver's door is still ajar. The sinking feeling I should have never materializes because my brain already connects the dots to a question I don't even have to ask. He must have wanted to try to get one last look as if to make sure he was quitting for the right reason. Idiot.

"Is he down there?" I call across the short distance once I have pushed my door open. I keep my gaze trained on what's going on outside of my windshield as I blindly search the glove compartment for the flashlight hidden amongst the clutter of receipts, napkins, spare gloves, a map and one or two esoteric books.

Whatever the answer is I don't hear it as much as I feel it, like something snaking through my brain and scratching with jagged nails. It tells me to hurry up and so I do.

By the time I have my gun drawn and have surveyed Cortland's car Reyes is standing right at the edge of the pit. Under the full moon the tips of his dress shoes glisten like polished stone as they hang recklessly over the lip.

He doesn't say a word to me, doesn't look at me either, just points down into the dark pit with a manicured nail. Flicking on my flashlight I throw the light over him and see exactly why he's been so strangely silent aside from the faint wet noise emitting from him. The muscles of his jaw work, relaxing and tightening against the large wad in his mouth. Whatever it is, it produces a steady stream of dark viscous fluid down the front of his coat. It takes longer than it should for me to understand that Reyes is chewing something. He's got the same manic look in his eyes again too.

Immediately I swing the beam of light down towards the salt pit and freeze.

It's down there.

Sitting on a mound of sand with the broken remains of Cortland hanging out of its mouth and chewing. But it looks worse than I remember. Not because it's an abomination undulating there under the glare of my light, but because the same black fluid smeared across Reyes' face and clothes is oozing out of a mangled right flank where what's left of a malformed arm twitches. At least that's what I think it is. Or rather was. It's hard to tell with the way the creature churns over the sand unwilling to stop what it's doing. My heart finds its way into my mouth when a host of eyes roll upwards and focuses on me.

Anything that I might say gets stuck in my throat and stays there even when Reyes spits into his hand.

It jingles, the thing he spits out. It jingles the way you expect too many metal charms and beads to do when they're all crowded together. My brain warns me about looking but my head turns anyway to watch as Reyes picks out half-chewed chunks of meat from between silver links. And then he holds up the item for us both to see, letting it catch in the moonlight. There, dangling from dirty fingers like a medal is a collection of random charms all attached to a simple link of metal rings. A bracelet.

My sister's bracelet.

"We found her."

Reyes' voice sounds too distant in my head as I taste metal from where the end of the flashlight now sits between my teeth, as I push bullet after bullet into the revolver's chambers. I aim down into the pit and fire. Once. Twice.

Somehow I get down there without too much mishap in the dark all the while aiming at the shrieking monstrosity that wiggles backwards, propelled on a nest of tails that whip and snap at the sand and salt that have become wet with the tide rushing in. For each two feet it clears I cut it in half and aim for one of the larger eyes. Another shot.

The last four shots aren't planned but it doesn't take me long to find out where I've aimed by the time the water has reached my shins. There's nothing left of what once had been my sister's face.

Someone starts screaming then, a terrible inhuman thing that hurts my ears, until it becomes a whimper and I reach up to cover my face. That's when Reyes joins me in the now black tinged water.

It's always been a personal rule to never watch him at work, but this time I do. Like Lola I can't give my sister a proper burial. Not with her looking like that. And so I let Reyes consume her completely before he moves on to the parts of Cortland that were left behind.

By the time I get back into my car, that cloying stench that has followed me for the past few weeks is gone. In its place is Reyes' distinct smell of aftershave and cigarette smoke as he crawls into my backseat and stretches out. That and bloody meat.

I turn the engine over thinking I'll finally be able to get some sleep tonight.

Our Best Selves

Hiron Ennes

THE HOUSE IS a squat trapezium of stone, fissured like the trunk of
a tree. Its cracked slab of a roof slumps under centuries of vines,
piebald with moss. When our cab approaches, a small owl rustles
from a window and flutters up to the canopy.

Mum takes to it right away. She stumbles from the taxi with the
cat in one arm and my brother in the other, leaving a trail of
dropped objects behind her. Dad tries to mirror her enthusiasm.
He picks up after her, snatching gloves and socks and booklets like
a hen pecking. He wears a patient smile until he gets to the doorway, where he finally sees the magnitude of his fixer-upper. The
floors are dirt. Leafy columns of light tumble through the cracks in
the roof. A possum hisses in the entryway.

His wife is nothing but pleased. She circles the house, examining crumbling furniture carved from the same stone as the walls.
Crude marble cylinders pass for stools. Slabs like tombstones mark
the headboards. My brother wipes dust from a windowsill to find it
trimmed in obsidian.

I slip through a fissure in the wall to the garden. Mum is
already out there, bending over the mossy quadrangles of stone.
She digs through the hardened earth, appraising the crumbling
soil. There are plenty of things already growing. Berries, shrubs,

apple trees, a couple of wild tubers. The canopy is thin, and there are soft patches where she can build more beds. Even the shady bits will be wrapped around her green thumb soon enough.

She rounds the stone fence and points out where she'll plant the spinach later this week. Where the beets will go, the tomatoes, her meticulously engineered squashes. She runs her boot through the brush, demarcating the beds, but my eyes have already wandered.

A sapling rustles by a window on the north side of the house. It's not an ash, not a maple, not an oak — its leaves, long and dark and strange, undulate in my direction. I know a greeting when I see it, so I step over to brush its bark, soft, smooth as skin, and dusted with fine green hairs.

"What's this one?" I ask Mum.

"I don't know, darling," she answers. "But I think it's yours."

THE FIRST NIGHT, we claim our rooms. If they can be called rooms. Some only become rooms when we drape Mum's tapestries over their missing walls. Others are completely closed in by vines writhing up from the floor. None has a door.

A fissure in the north wall widens into a sort of window, looking out on the sapling. I want the bed closest to it, but my brother gets there first. I decide to fight him for it, and neither of us will budge. He's got his eye on that tree, and he doesn't believe me when I say it's mine.

In the end, Mum claims the room for herself and Dad. She says it's because she does not want to see us fight over it. She tells us that when we are squabbling, we are not our best selves, and we must always strive to be our best selves.

Dad lays their blankets down over the bed-slab and agrees.

"When you think about it, your mother and I are the unlucky ones," he says. "This is the only room that doesn't have a view of that beautiful night sky."

A WEEK IN, Dad takes his axe on a foray into the woods. He's decided that before he can install the floor panels, carve doors and shutters and repair Mum's loom, and especially before the rain comes, he must fix the roof.

My brother and I find pieces of it scattered around the property. We're supposed to be finishing our schoolwork, but we circle the yard, cutting away ferns and unburying dozens of wide, broken wedges. They lie scattered in every direction — a few have fallen so far that the cat won't follow us out to them, preferring to sit and yowl in the doorway. My brother wants to gather the missing pieces and fit the roof back together like a puzzle. He quickly learns that none of us could lift the smallest fragment.

"How did the roof break, anyway?" he asks me.

"Earthquake," I say, because I can't think of anything else with enough force.

He goes silent for a while, watching Dad pile his cuts at the edge of the garden, thin trunks that look similar to pine but smell much sweeter. Sap dark as mud oozes from their axe-bites.

"How was the house even built?" my brother asks.

"There's mountains nearby," I answer. "The builders chipped off slabs and carried them down here."

"Why?" He gestures to the trees, a verdant abundance of beams and floorboards and shingles. "And *how*?"

"They were giants," I answer. "It was easy for them. This is just their dollhouse."

"No, it's not."

"I'm serious. We're their dolls. Once they know we're here, they'll come play with us. Put you in a little dress, snap your limbs off."

I've gone a step too far. He frowns and floats over to Mum, who's planting her greens in neat, straight rows. He leans up to her, and she shakes her head.

"Don't lie to your brother," she hollers. "Those who lie are not at their best."

I sigh and look to the sapling at the end of the garden. It shudders and waves, though there's no wind I can feel.

~

THE CAT IS NO LONGER STRICTLY an outdoor cat, since there are no longer strict outdoors. He wanders through the fractures of the house day and night, chattering, kneading, marking.

Dad says he can't get the smell of piss out of his nose. He wonders aloud if he should abandon the roof and prioritize making doors.

"He's a pest," Dad says.

"He's the only reason why we're not overrun with rodents," Mum answers. She skins a few tubers at the sink, paring knife glinting with remarkable speed.

"At least let's keep him out of our room. He makes you wheeze."

"He doesn't —" she stops herself. She's not going to say the cat doesn't make her wheeze, not after what she's just told me about lying.

"And the hives," Dad says. "Your condition worries me as it is."

Mum gives him an irritated frown. "I don't have a condition," she answers, slowly, each word a careful guess.

She sets down her tubers and retreats to the garden, where she walks along her fresh rows for the rest of the evening. She doesn't even come in for dinner, after I have finished the paring and Dad the boiling, when my brother has set our stone table with stone plates. For hours, she paces and mutters among her seedlings. She is praying fervently, and against Dad's wishes, for rain.

EVERY WOMAN in our family has exactly one daughter. There are no sisters, no cousins, no childless maids, so our family tree is a thin, straight vine. All our knowledge of horticulture and herbalism descends in this way, unbroken and perfectly linear. The genealogies of our squashes are far more tangled.

My mother has already taught me most of it. She taught me which plants are friends and which aren't, which to eradicate and which to cultivate, which animals are pests and which tinctures might kill them. She taught me how to skin a tree, to soak and dry and flatten its pulp into paper, how to prune a tomato's limbs so the others proliferate unimpeded, how to select for traits that help our lineages grow into their best selves.

Despite her teachings, I can't identify the plant that has grown at the foot of my bed. A collection of dew has sprinkled through the hole in my ceiling, coaxing a green shoot from the ground. Overnight it's crawled up the granite slab of my mattress.

When I poke my head into Mum's room, telling her I've found something new, she says she's feeling faint. She's tucked in bed with the cat and neither are willing to move. She'll hold out for as long as she can, until the blankets are soaked and we have to clean up the blood.

"Make me my tea," she says.

I retreat to the kitchen and grab her jar of little red pills. I steep them with the rest of the leaves while she groans in her room, more frustrated than pained. She's been trying for so long to wean herself off the stuff, the same way she's weaned off every medicine that came before. I hate the tea, but not because it smells like rot and looks worse, but because I am afraid, one day, that I'll need it too.

DAD COMES home with what he thinks is a boar but what may be something else. It's four-legged and hairless, long neck sagging on his back as he trundles back to the house. We help him drag it to the porch and watch him get to work with his knife.

"It's been so long since I've had any meat," he says, elbow-deep in blood. "My poor belly's sagging." He slaps his navel, leaving a splattered red print.

"We'll have you fed properly when the garden comes in," Mum tells him. "You just have to wait."

"Time is a necessity," I say.

"And what else?" Mum asks, smiling.

"Rain, sun and soil," my brother says, "are the only necessities."

"Very good."

The blood drips from the porch into the garden, where the early squashes grasp skyward. The sapling stands nearby, branches brushing the half-finished awning. Either it's grown taller in the past couple days, or it's gotten closer.

~

DAD MANAGES to patch the roof by the first rains. It starts as a gentle patter, then, early in the morning, becomes a downpour. We are jolted awake by a deep, resounding snap, far closer than thunder. The house shudders with the echo of the rumble, and we all crawl from our beds.

In the kitchen, we find a pool of water, whirling around notches of wood and stone. Above our heads, a new fissure bolts through the ceiling, zagging from the hearth to the table. Dust and rain fall from the crack, pattering against our firewood.

Dad rolls a stool under the breach. He blinks through the thin sheet of sky-lit water, then lifts himself up to the crack. We clutch our nightgowns and watch his hand disappear into the fissure. He stills for a moment, frowns, then pulls a thin, long vine from the crack. He wraps it around his wrist, then his arm. Soon it's curling at his feet, yards and yards of leafless green.

When he finally snaps it from the crack, he's soaked. I'm not sure if it's rainwater or sweat.

~

"THE CAT IS BAD FOR YOU," Dad says. "We need to get rid of it."

"Don't you dare," Mum replies, wiping her nose. She is bedridden again today. "It's just the season. The pollen. It's gotten so thick."

She's not wrong. Gold dust has settled in with early summer, falling like snow through our open windows. Our sideboard, a recent project Dad painstakingly carved from oak, hasn't shown its surface in days. When we close our schoolbooks, we do so in puffs of yellow powder.

"He makes your eyes water," Dad says. "He wrecks your lungs —"

"He doesn't." If Mum wasn't already lulled by her tea, she would notice how badly she's lying. But she is not her best. Her face is pale and dotted with sweat.

"It's not the pollen," Dad continues. "You know it — that animal is bad for your health, and your health is the whole reason we're out here."

"My health was an excuse," Mum replies. "You're happy here."

Dad's breath softens, his pause heavy. "Sure."

~

A FIRE BURNS in the hearth. The flames flicker blue and cold, so Dad gets another log. It slumps, soft and wet, like the last three.

"We shouldn't burn those," I say. "They're moldy."

He doesn't seem to hear me. "God," he breathes. "What I wouldn't give for a beer."

"Mum will kill you if you go back to town."

"Just for a night, dear." He glances at me. "You don't miss it?"

I shrug. I don't, really — I don't miss the old house, with its tiny garden. The school. The hospital. All the things that held us back, before Mum decided she didn't need it anymore — not the medicine or the car or the money to pay for any of it. Her best self would never need anything but sun and soil and rain and time.

Soft sobbing comes from the hallway. We turn from the fire to see Mum in her bloodstained nightgown, out of bed for the first time in three days. Her eyes are red, her cheeks flushed and wet. The cat dangles in her arms.

"Look at him," she says. "Something's wrong. Look."

She lays the creature on the kitchen table. The pollen clings to his fur and cakes his bloodied nose. She tries to stand him up, but he wobbles and falls, yellows of his eyes swallowed by the round, reflective black pools of his pupils.

"He looks toxic," Dad says.

"Did you give him something?" Mum asks. "Did you do something to him?"

"Of course not."

She begins to cry.

"I didn't do anything," Dad says. "Just wait. He might get better."

Mum wipes her swollen eyes, fingers goopy with pollen-stuff. "This is your fault."

"It's not."

"I'm going to find out how you did it," she says. She skirts the table, pulling jars of medicines from the shelf, opening stone drawers to rattle stone utensils. "I'll find it. I'll find what you gave him."

"I didn't give him anything!"

She ignores him, moving through the kitchen, the bedrooms, the back porch. She pulls books from their cases, and then pages from their spines. She digs through my schoolwork, breaks my pens and empties them, she dumps her jars of herbs and spices and preserves onto the counter.

She finds nothing amiss. She knows best what plants and oils go where, medicinal and toxic, which might dissolve harmlessly in a human mouth but fester in an animal's. She knows every leaf, seed and extract; Dad does not.

She gives up. Sobbing, she leaves the cat on the table and returns to her room. A thin trail of blood remains, smeared by the hem of her dress.

~

A DAY LATER, while Dad buries the cat, the oak handle of his shovel breaks in half.

~

IT's an insult to describe my tree as a sapling anymore. Its trunk has thickened, its leaves fan out to arm's length. Its roots are flexible, growing, alive with tiny creaks and groans of xylem, billions of invisible stretching grains. If I listen hard enough, I can hear the soil shift between its rhizomes.

In a span of a few days, it overtakes the cat's grave. It lingers on that spot for a week, filling its roots, then slowly, slowly, retreats to the garden. It takes a month for it to make it from the lettuce beds to the tomatoes.

A little sentinel, Mum calls it. She no longer cries every day. Her breathing is clear. She has begun to make paper again.

Pulp floats on the surface of her soaking tub. She stirs it by hand, letting the bloated sludge drip through her fingers. It's a familiar task, a familiar smell, but today I find it oddly sickening.

A deep boom shakes the house, rippling the tub. Neither of us flinch. We are no longer startled by the crack of breaking stone.

Even with the rains gone, every night we dream of new fissures, and wake to the sun shining through them.

Then, the crumbling of stone transforms, rising in pitch and severity until I realize it's not stone at all. My brother is screaming.

We abandon the soaking paper and stumble down the hall. A buzz of terror rustles the ferns peeking through the cracks in our walls.

A massive wedge of the roof occupies the center of the room. A broken portion of marble angles down from a streak of bare night sky, stone splinted with long planks of Dad's repair work. The dead wood has rotted, choked under a burden of leaves and branches and vines. Stems sway along the debris, swollen with sap, a shivering mass of rot and stone and greenery so convoluted I can't tell where it ends and my brother begins.

Dad appears behind us. He cries out, digging through the wreckage, grasping at his weeping, trapped son. I help him tear at the vines, snapping branches, ripping away sheets of bark. My brother finally appears again, mostly intact. His right arm is inextricable, and he screams every time our father tries to unearth it.

"Don't —" he wails. "Don't touch it — *don't!*"

Silent, mustering an uncanny strength, Dad pushes the slab off my brother's elbow.

Mum hugs me as her son rises from the debris, face bloody, arm hanging limp and mangled by his side. Patches of skin curl away like birch bark. He's got two new elbows, tipped with protuberances of white bone. Leaves and pinecone scales stick to his wounds. There is a splinter the size of a penknife lodged in his shoulder.

He is too shocked to cry out as Dad grips him under the knees and lifts him into his arms.

"I can fix him," Mum says. "It's bad, but I can do it. He needs a salve. He needs poultice — wait here, I can fix him."

"No, you can't," Dad barks. "He needs a hospital. He needs a fucking doctor."

"We can't —"

Dad shoves past her, terrified son in his arms. He carries him down the hall without looking at either of us, stomps through the kitchen, pushes open the front door.

"*Don't!*" Mum shouts. "He'll be fine! Please, we can do this ourselves. We *have* to do this ourselves!"

"We don't, and we can't," Dad growls. "I'm taking him to town."

Rapidly, my brother's shock abates, just enough to make room for dawning horror. He trembles, rustling the leaves sprouting from his mangled arm.

"I don't want to go back," he sobs. "Put me down. I want to stay."

"Listen to him!" Mum says. "Please, he's fine."

"I don't wanna leave!" my brother shouts, but Dad marches on.

"You can't just *walk* there!" Mum hollers, trailing him all the way to the squashes, to the moss-eaten path of pebbles that passes for a road.

Dad keeps walking, dodging the words flung at him, and with his arms clamped around my brother, disappears into the night.

~

I DON'T SLEEP that night. Neither does Mum. I crawl into bed with her, curling like the cat, and she moans until dawn.

In the morning, she works in the garden, violently pruning the tomatoes. She cracks stem after stem, nursing her cold tea in an obsidian mug. It doesn't help.

"It's good for the plants," she says, when I point out she's leaving a trail of blood. "It's nutrient rich." Then she begins to cry. Her tears drip thick and white like sap down her face.

"They're not coming back," she says.

"They are."

"The hospital will keep him — they'll put him down. My boy, my little boy. They'll murder him like your bastard father murdered the cat."

"Dad didn't murder the cat."

While she sobs, I try to clean the garden with the scuffle hoe, but it seems cruel, impossible. I try to sweep, but the cracked broom is heavy in my hands. I try to dry the paper, but the pulp repulses me. Every object seems to me a desiccated, desecrated corpse.

~

TWO MORE DAYS PASS. Then, they return. They have three arms between them.

My brother teeters, unsteady, wrapped in strips of his blood-stained pajamas. The severed sleeves of our father's coat bind his wound. He waves with his good arm from the end of the path, smiling through his pallor.

Mum, revitalized, rushes out to greet him, wrapping her arms around him and nearly lifting him from the ground. He groans when her chin brushes against his raw bud of a shoulder.

Dad greets Mum with a quick peck to the forehead. He looks like he's slept about as much as we have.

"What happened?" Mum asks. "Did the hospital just...let you go?"

"We never got that far," Dad admits. He eases himself through the front door and collapses on the stone table. "We had to stop."

Mum waits for an explanation. Dad is already half-asleep, curling his knees into his chest and closing his eyes.

She shakes him back awake. "What happened?"

He blinks. "We had to stop. I couldn't make it that far. We found a stream. I cleaned him up."

"Where'd his arm go?" I ask.

"I...pulled it off," Dad says. He turns over, buries his face in his hands, and releases something halfway between a laugh and a sob. "Snapped. Twisted it like a branch. It came right off."

"It did," says my brother proudly.

"Oh, my dears," Mum says, kissing them both. "I knew you could do it all by yourselves. I'm so proud of you. I knew you wouldn't give up."

Dad's breathing slows. "I...buried it," he mumbles. "By the stream."

Then he drifts away, exhausted from his travels. He's a sturdy man, rooted to the ground — he isn't meant to wander like that.

My brother is famished. While Dad snores on the table, he eats on the floor, chewing through the last of our early vegetables. He asks when the squashes will grow in. He asks if we cried when he got hurt. He asks if he can go dig up his arm later.

Mum laughs, tells him no. You should never unearth what you've already planted.

~

DAD CONFESSES it's probably for the best they never made it to town. "It would've cost an arm and a leg to save that arm," he laughs. "Though I might've been tempted to get them to do something about this belly. It's sagging over my belt. In a few weeks I'll start tripping over it."

"When the squashes come in," Mum says, "we'll fatten you back up. We'll put some flesh under there." Her tone is earnest; by the silhouettes my parents cast against the ferns growing from the walls, they're holding one another close.

Dad blows an amused puff from his nose. The shadow of his arm reaches for her, skin hanging like a curtain from his elbow.

"You're breathing better," he says. "It really was that cat."

"Oh, stop."

"He was bad for you. He wasn't letting you grow into your best self."

"I know," Mum says. Then, quietly: "He was a pest."

I smile and look through the fissured ceiling to my tree, its dark crown spreading over our house like a new roof. I can feel its roots move under the floor, absorbing the activity inside. I can feel its soft, hairy bark brush up against the walls, soaking up my parents' heat, my brother's quiet, musical moans. His stub aches, but only with the pressure of new growth.

I shudder, relieved, contented. Leaves rustle in the breeze above me.

∾

AUTUMN COMES heavy and full and fast.

The squashes swell with meat. The tomatoes burst and spill seeds, too heavy for their branches. The greens bolt, the wild apples fall, the corn shoots upward. Everything has grown to painful fullness, fecund and aching for relief.

My mother and I return to the kitchen with skirts full of vegetables. The peas are big as beets, the beets big as melons, the melons too big to carry. My father rolls one onto the porch, where he slices and salts and cans, swearing when he pinches his loose skin in the jar lids.

"Fucking tongs," he says, attempting to wrangle his chopped cantaloupe. "Everything wood in this goddamn house breaks."

My brother takes the utensils from him, extending his unbroken arm. It has grown a little longer, a little stronger in the absence of the other. He still likes using it, though two new ones have grown from his stub, stocky and thick. With his long arm he carries the tongs to the garden edge, with his short ones he digs a second grave, next to the cat's, and buries them.

Dad attempts to replace the tongs by whittling away at a

branch of alder, but I can tell it unnerves him as much as it does me. We can both feel the pinch of steel scraping at the wood, hear the grain snapping and curling in pain. After a while, he gives up, blaming the skin hanging from between his fingers.

I tell him to make a new set of utensils out of bone.

"Whose bones?" he laughs. Then he stops, thinking over what I've said. The river isn't too far. It might take a day to get there and back.

Soon, the whole weight of the garden hits us. The squashes fill to bursting, agonized, stretched skin splitting open and spilling their entrails. Mum has to carry them in pieces to the kitchen, handful after handful of raw, ripe meat. I pluck the tomatoes while my brother makes his rounds of the garden, long arm reaching for what the rest of us can't. He strips the highest cobs from the corn, gathers seeds from the sunflowers, shakes loose the apples. Dad marches behind him, gathering the spoils in the loose apron of his stomach. When he can't carry any more, when his skin stretches with the bounty, he dumps the spoils onto our kitchen table.

My brother quickly sorts through them, organizing with respect to size and type and ripeness. The haul is so large it doesn't matter that he slips the cherry tomatoes into his mouth when Mum isn't looking, or nibbles at the basil stems. He is a growing boy. A fourth arm, short and soft as a baby's, juts sidelong from one of his new elbows.

Mum removes seeds from the squash, digging her fingers through the orange meat and passing around sticky handfuls. We can only get through a quarter of it before we are too full to move.

Outside, the sky is cold and clear and blue. The deciduous leaves darken and shed, readying for the next turn of the season.

When the harvest is done and we've gathered all we can, Mum lies out in the empty garden, wetting the soil and steeping it for the following year. She can't stop grinning as she feeds the garden, lying in each patch and bleeding for a few hours before moving onto the next. Wordless, hair rustling in the breeze, her voice carries like birdsong through the house.

We've done it, she says. We've finally done it.

~

WINTER IS BLISS.

On the nights we make paper, Dad sits on a marble stool while my brother grasps his skin, stretching it across the kitchen. I run a paring knife along it, trimming the hair, then through it. We cut a generous length from him, then I pat the laceration down with a compress of leaves and soil. Soon Dad stops gritting his teeth. He tells me it feels nice. He's always wanted to lose weight.

We pull his skin taut over a frame of bones, scrape off the pulp of his fat, and dry it in the cold sun. When the snows come, we stretch it over the ceiling, we hang it from doorways, we throw it over the beds and pillows and curl in its warmth. My book covers are stretched from his fingers. Our front door is made from his belly, navel protruding where a knob may have been. I have never loved him more.

When we are hungry, my brother lifts his long arm and reaches down the hallway, into the back room, where he grabs hold of dried corn and beans, or he rolls around a rock-hard squash, making a game of it. His arm is too long to reach his own mouth, and his other ones get mixed up with one another, so Mum breaks apart his food for him. For every morsel she brings to his lips, she scatters ten at his feet.

Occasionally, he will get bored. If I don't watch my back, I'll feel a tap on my shoulder or a tug at my clothes, and when I turn, I'll catch a glimpse of his long, pale arm snaking back into his room. I've never seen him grin as widely as he does when he pulls my hair from across the house. Sometimes, he snaps it off like a bunch of twigs, though always, more will grow.

The sapling has taken up residence right outside my room, branches stretching through the window, roots curling up from the floor. I don't think it can move much anymore, but it seems content, bathing in the beige light shining through the tapestries of skin.

~

I SIT IDLY MOST of these days, arms splayed under the lengthening daylight. Weeks pass before any of us become hungry or bored, months before my father grows a new length of skin to cut and dry and use again. There is little to do, but none of us mind. We want for nothing. We need nothing, except time, rain, sun and soil.

Stopping Places

Nelson Stanley

RADIE SAYS: Secrets are heavy.

Radie says: We think that by keeping them to ourselves — by struggling alone under all that weight — we can make them safe.

Radie says: We think, if we can just bear up under the load, everything will be fine. But really, your silence is there just to protect yourself.

Radie says: We are a secret now. You and me. You see? We've shared it, so we've halved the weight.

I shake my head, which appears to be filled with static and cobwebs.

Which one are you again? I say.

She just smiles, and behind her, in the dark, something skitters across the floor.

THE WINTER my mother's Aunt Radie died we went to stop with her family down on the coast. In the grim week before New Year my mother, father and I piled in to our rusting Ford van and puttered down the winding roads to the Kent seaside. That winter the roads close to where they lived were spattered and lined with roadkill, shattered corpses lying almost neatly along the verges, piled on the edges of the pavement. Mostly rabbits — bigger than I'd ever seen before, twisted trails of viscera webbed out behind them — but also badgers smushed to a grey-red blur, foxes with their hindquarters round the wrong way, crushed skulls and popped eyes. I tried to keep count of each animal, naming them as I did so — *Look! That's a fox!* — but after a couple of miles my old man snapped at me to shut up, and soon enough I lost count anyway.

My mother's cousin — also named Radie, and her daughter too; Romany Travellers are not known for our originality when it comes to handing out names — had married a man who owned a carpet business. My mother's cousin and the man she married lived in a static caravan that they called "the chalet," laid up in the gravelled car-park of the grotty prefab that served as the carpet warehouse, connected to it by umbilical lines delivering gas and electricity.

My father parked our little blue van next to their brand-new Mercedes SL, a dream in muted champagne.

He looked across at the car, then turned to me and said:

"For fuck's sake, don't show us up."

My mother and her cousin retreated to the kitchen to make tea. My father and Radie's husband sat and made stilted small talk about how bad business had been in the past year.

My cousin Radie stole me away to her room, to show me what she'd got for Christmas: great piles of dolls and accessories, a deluge of pink and sparkly plastic. She brought each toy out of its box with something like reverence, but seemed somehow confused by her ownership of them: after I'd *oohed* and *ahhed* over each, she took it roughly from me and threw it on the bed. Soon, her diffidence or my jealousy spoiled what vicarious pleasure there was in her haul, and, kicking a Barbie or Sindy off the side of her bed, I said:

"Did you get all this because your gran's just died?"

Her hair was frosted into puffy golden waves; her frock was some sort of chequered lacy thing, overdone frills with a bow on the front: box-fresh. My hair was pulled back into the tight ponytail I have worn ever since girlhood, though I'd been forced out of my Trevor Francis tracksuit and into a plaid skirt and woollen jumper for the occasion.

"No. Are you *dinlo* or something? I always get what I want."

My mother called us back to the front room, where the adults had settled down over the dregs of Christmas leftovers. The conversation turned to the dead. At the mention of her mother, her daughter welled up and began to tell us, in a cracking voice, of her mother's final agonies: raving, a descent into senility, loss of bodily control.

My father caught my eye and rolled his, a square hard man easily embarrassed by bodily functions, female troubles, emotions.

"She went on so, at the end," said Radie's husband.

"She was in a lot of pain," said my mother.

"They get lost," said my mother's cousin.

"Didn't know where she was," said her husband.

"She saw death coming."

"Well. She did always have a touch of the sight," said my mother.

"She were touched by *something*," said Radie's husband. He grinned, looked around for an audience, found none, and stopped grinning.

"What do you mean, *the sight?*"

"Little girls should be seen and not heard," said my father.

"She saw Alfie's death coming."

"Don't talk jank."

"She did. She told him not to get up on the roof. Said it was too windy. Told him. He never listened, though."

"See?"

"See what?"

"She was in a lot of pain towards the end, mind."

"She did love the countryside, though. Mum was so happy when we stopped down here."

"Reckon it was all the *shooshnis*." Her husband pointed at where my little cousin sat, in a big recliner by the sliding window. "Mad for 'em, she was. Sat there in that chair and watched them all day if you let her alone, and you'd think some of 'em was tamed the way they'd come right up to the window. I swear one day I saw a big bastard *baro*, big enough to scare the dog, come right up to her when she had that patio window open. Ate from her hand it did! I never seen nothing else like it. Ran off when I opened the door."

My old man looked confused.

"*Shooshnis* don't run, they hop."

"He don't mean *shooshni. Konengri,*" said my mother's cousin.

I blinked, half-used to being shown up by my relatives because they could *rokke* better than I could, but flummoxed all the same.

"He means *hares,*" said my cousin.

"Vermin's vermin," Radie's husband said. "They die the same way."

For a moment, my cousin's face clouded, as if she suffered a sudden pain. Then she brightened.

"Can we go outside and play?"

"Mind you come back for tea."

We put on our coats and my cousin dragged me outside, into the drizzle. Then, across the gravel forecourt, out down the twisting lanes — half-choked with sopping brambles and thorny gorse just coming in to flower — that led to the beach.

Her mother's voice followed us, from inside the chalet against the banging of the door:

"If the tide comes in and you get stuck and drowneded all to death, I shall be most upset."

HE'S NOT EVEN REALLY your father, Radie says.

I nod. There appears to be something fluttering in the meat of my brain, like a bird trapped in a room.

Wait, I say. Don't you mean *your* father?

She smiles like a trap closing over your leg, like a snare tightening, something you'll never get free of.

Radie says: Little leveret, you have so much to learn.

WE SHIVERED in the cold and the drizzle past a string of salt-corroded bungalows, past a closed-down tea-room with cheap aluminium chairs stacked on the veranda and chained up like dogs. We crashed through wet marram and saw-grass, past old signs warning of unexploded munitions, into the boggy grey of the dunes.

I chased my cousin through the scrub, one or the other of us taking turns to shriek with delight as we splashed and stumbled.

Radie turned towards the shore and led us scrambling up the dunes, wet sand crumbling under our feet. At the top, out of breath, I stood gaping at the vast flat plain of mud lolling out to sea between headlands where the crumbling loess of the cliffs fell away to reveal chalk beneath.

Thin gauzy light lay like a film over everything. Criss-crossing runnels scarred the mud all the way from the ill-looking tide to the edge of the dunes. Something about those channels mesmerised me: clogged here and there with a splotch of sad rubbery wrack, they looked like black snaking tentacles flowing out of the water and across the mud. Some were thin ribbons and some seemed to be wide enough to lie down in, gouged out of the beach. I tried to imagine what could possibly have caused them.

"It's the worms," said Radie, close by my ear.

"What?" I said, without turning round.

"The worms. Huge ones. That's what makes those lines in the sand. Enormous worms. They come up out of the sea, dragging their great wormery bulk with them, and they hunt down little *chavis* who've been bad."

The brown tide churned against the brown mud. Drizzle fell out of a cold grey sky.

"Was never worms," I said, not very confidently, staring at the beach.

"Was."

"Was not."

"Can prove it."

"How?"

"Their young'uns. They'll getcha, if you stay still too long."

The wind got up, shrieking across the rotting sea, lashing foam against the mud.

A cold wetness at the back of my neck, something blind and questing as it slipped down inside my jumper. As they writhed down my back, oleaginous yet gritty from where they'd been torn from the sand, I shrieked and pulled at my clothing, caught between ramming a hand down my collar and shoving a hand up inside my hem to fish them out.

My sob-choked howls mingled with Radie's near-hysterical peals of laughter. She turned and ran off back down the dunes, into the scrub. She got a good head-start: I spent a good five minutes writhing and clawing at myself, filled with the keening horror that one of my new passengers would slip up my arse and make its nest inside me.

I tore off after her, determined to inflict revenge any way I could.

∽

RADIE SAYS: He'd go out and kill them, looking for the right one. Goes out at night with an air-rifle, sets poison, swerves his car whenever he sees something crossing the road. He knew I was in them — part of me was in them — so he kills them. Lays them down by the roadside, as if that'd fool anyone.

Radie says: People always think that you can kill a thing and that's the end of it.

I say: They do?

I want to say so many other things, but it's getting so hard to think.

Radie says: They do. But my little leveret, there's things waiting *everywhere*. You just have to know where to look.

∽

FURTHER ALONG THE BEACH — tucked back about a hundred yards from the dunes, nestling in the lee of the embankment that supported the road — there was a line of squat concrete structures tilting into the sand and marram, facing in the direction of the sea: roughly hexagonal, pierced at intervals by holes like large letter-boxes let into the concrete.

I stuck my hands into the rough openings of the first and tried to haul myself up, to see inside, but I wasn't tall enough or strong enough. Its concrete skin was split and weathered by the sea air, by the ravages of time. The edges of the roof were cracked and spalled, showing dirty orange-brown stains where the rebar was showing through from underneath.

I tried to shout my cousin's name, but my voice came out

cracked and small and was blown away by the wind. Something moved off to my right, quicksilver loping movement, the sawgrass rattling as it rounded the concrete structure away from me, squeezing between the embankment and the wall.

I thought:

That's a big dog.

Then I thought:

That's a *person*. On all fours.

Then I thought:

People don't have fur.

I should have been frightened then, I suppose. But I wanted to find Radie and I couldn't remember the way back to the chalet on my own, so I pushed back the wet sawgrass and inched around the side of the little concrete building, squeezed between the rear of it and the embankment shoring up the road, scrambled around the back.

At the back was a door-size hole, shrunken by subsidence and nearly choked with rubbish: soft drink and beer bottles and cans bleached by sea and wind, thick tangled hanks of what looked like hair, brittle and old, a scree of pebbles and delicate shells and a large clutch of dead-man's fingers, dotted here and there with strangled shellfish, rotting to a sickly brownish-red. It smelled like a clogged and overflowing drain, thick and sulphurous. From the embankment songbirds screamed and chirruped like there was a storm coming. A pheasant sent up a rattle of warning.

I ignored it, and stepped inside.

An interior wall ran left to right, making a sort of corridor. I felt my way along, hands held out in front of me, then slipped through the gap between the wall and the structure's outer skin.

Inside the bunker proper, the grey light of afternoon dripped weakly through the embrasures. No rubbish littered the concrete of the floor, and no graffiti defaced its cracked cement walls. What I took to be a small, long-dead dog was laid out in the centre of the floor. Then I took in its long tattered ears, the length and power of its legs, and realised it was the corpse of a hare, fur patchy through decomposition, dry eye huge in its socket.

Next to it, Radie knelt on the gritty concrete, stroking the threadbare fur on the dead thing's flank: long, gentle strokes, starting up between the ears and tracing its spine down to the ragged bobble of its tail. As I got closer, I realised her mouth was moving, but no words were coming out.

I called her name; my voice quavered back off the concrete. I tried again.

"Radie, what are you doing? Why are you touching that filthy thing?"

"I need to get away," she said.

"Then let's go back to the chalet."

I stepped closer. The hare had been slit cleanly down the belly: the fur and the greaseproof-paper skin underneath had been folded back in a neat square flap and the organs had been scooped out from inside.

"Don't be putting that down my blouse now, Radie," I said. "I'm not afraid of you."

Her head snapped round like she'd just noticed I was there.

"You should be," she said, in a voice that was not hers. "If I was you, *I* would be. Aren't I lucky?"

"Lucky? Why?"

"Because I'm not you."

"Of course you're not me. What a silly thing to say."

"I need your help," Radie said.

I wrinkled my nose.

"It smells in here. We should get back."

"Give me your hand."

"Not if you're going to put worms down me again."

She smiled, and I was afraid.

"No worms. Not this time. Before, it was like treacle," she said, hollowly but in conversational tones. "And before that, it was like...you know the way sand gets blown off the edge of a dune? Ever watched that? The way it falls sideways and...over itself, I mean. Like that. On top of me, like that."

She touched her left shoulder with her right hand, then quickly down and across herself to her opposite hip. The other hand continued to stroke the empty corpse of the hare.

"I don't know what you're talking about. Let's go back to the chalet. We can play with your dolls —"

The gloom in that bunker intensified, seemed to thicken.

"I have to lift it off of me," she said, in her awful faraway voice. "Now you're here, you can help."

A slight crawling feeling inside the back of my neck, the thick cord of nerves inside its brittle sheath of bone stirring, of its own volition. Outside, the birds stopped singing.

"Help? How?"

"Give me your hand. It won't hurt."

I reached out. Her hand was freezing. The wind soughed through the gun-slits. The hair on my arms stirred and lifted. My ears popped.

"Do you know what you are, my girl?"

I nodded; I shook my head.

"They tell us we steal their children," she said, her voice coming as if from inside a deep well. She began to sing, her voice echoing up from depths:

"My mother said, I never should
Play with the Gypsies in the wood..."

She stopped singing and laughed, a terrible sound.

"Yet it's our babbies that they take away from their parents, into care and into orphanages. It's us who grow up never knowing our own. It's us who grow up with nothing but lies about who we are and where we come from.

"When I was a *chavi*," she said, "the gavvers came to our stopping-place. Told us a baby had been took from the town. They went through the trailers, one by one. Mothers, the ailing — we all had to stand outside in the rain while they searched. Me mum told us not to look 'em in the eye, for if you look a gavver in the eye they think you're gonna fight back, and then they'd take us away."

I opened my mouth to speak but there was no air in my lungs, no sound now, no light. I felt like I was being crushed under an enormous weight. There was just her voice, droning on and on in that bunker on a drear afternoon at the end of the world.

Cold, then heat, round the back of my neck.

The weight on my chest, slipping slowly across me.

The hare, now whole, twitched, scrabbled with all four feet on the floor — a quick, shocked movement, more reflex than volition — then skittered away shaking its narrow head. Its huge ears waggled comically. The hare struggled to the gap in the edge of the wall as if it hadn't worked out quite how to use its legs; there, in the rough-hewn concrete entrance-way, it paused, looked back at us watching it. It quivered its nostrils, sat back on its hind legs, pawed frantically at its face like a person who'd just walked through a veil of cobwebs and was desperate to scrape them off. Then it turned, and was gone.

"When you've been down here as long as I have, you'll know better than to follow hares," she said, and I was lost.

To the Wolves

Sasha Brown

THE ANCIENT MAN's face a crumpled paper ball. Skin fragile as toilet paper; a thick dark scab on one cheek, loose at a corner. Pale eyes unfocused, mouth hanging open.

He wore a gray bathrobe, threadbare and stained, and he was blocking the doorway to the common area. His arms quivered thin as a model's: braced on a walker, but he did not walk.

Behind him, in a narrow hallway peeling with frog-green paint, Louscha reached a fluttering hand just short of his shoulder. She was old, but not as old as him. She was wearing a pantsuit, dressed up for her first day. "Sir?" she ventured. "Sir, I'm afraid you're blocking the way."

Her son hovered behind her, flustered and full of tension. He wore a faded old Bates t-shirt. The old man seemed to agitate him. "Sir, you can't just block the doorway," he finally said, pushing by the old man with perhaps more force than he'd intended. The man staggered and almost fell, but — as though kicked into gear by the push — began to shuffle away.

"I'm so sorry," Louscha said after him, casting a sharp look at her son. "Stephan, that wasn't kind."

But Stephan was gazing around him, distracted and dismayed. "I don't think he even noticed," he muttered. "God, Mom, this place is…"

The common room was a great high-ceilinged cavern, big and echoey. It had been a gymnasium once. Now, dust hung lazy in the yellow air. Big glass block windows dropped light onto shoals of shuffling elders. The rubbery pocking of their walkers echoed against the cinderblock walls. Sagging armchairs and sofas were strewn around, elders sunk in like ingrown hairs. They didn't move. Some stared straight at the ceiling, mouths agape like baby birds.

"It's terrible," said Stephan. "Mom, it's not too late to back out. I don't — this isn't nice enough. It doesn't feel right."

"Don't be silly," she said, patting his arm. "You're just not used to seeing so many old people in one place. Look, they're not all so out of it." She nodded her chin towards a table of seniors playing cards. They, at least, were well-dressed and healthy looking. One, with a bouffant that could only be a wig, looked pointedly back as though appraising her. Louscha waved. "My darling, I know the sacrifices you made to get me in here. Your home equity loan...I'm grateful. I'm sure I'll be quite happy here." But she stayed close to him.

"I barely did anything," Stephan protested, "not compared to the sacrifices you've made for me." It had always been just the two of them, since he was a little kid. She'd never dated; she worked two jobs. He'd meant to become rich and buy her a house, but he hadn't quite managed it. "Come on. We can live together in my condo. It'll be fun."

He didn't really want that, and both of them knew it. Louscha tsked. "Balderdash. How would you find a new wife with me doddering about? You must be free, Stephy. Free to find love. Maybe a girl who comes with children you could grow to love, too." She stroked his arm. "I wouldn't want you to do anything more. This place is just fine. And besides, it's the duty of each generation —"

She was cut off by an awful shriek. A woman across the room rocked furiously in her wheelchair. "I don't belong here!" she shrieked, and the chair tipped over, sprawling her across the floor. "This isn't me! Let me out! This isn't me!" She beat her fists against the floor like a child in impotent anger, until an orderly knelt next to her. A needle flashed; she went limp, and was set back in her chair and wheeled away.

"She's got no marbles up there at all, poor dear." The bouffanted woman had come up behind them. "Keeping her quiet and peaceful is the kindest they can do for her now, I'm afraid." Her lip curled, as though she was amused. "I'm Claudia. It's your first day, isn't it? Come and sit with us. We're not all doddering ninnies here, you know. Come!"

Louscha smiled bravely, and they followed Claudia across the echoing floor. "Did they tell you this used to be the gymnasium? A little odd for a common area now, but it allows us to congregate. This was a boarding school, once. Eons ago. It's been a retirement home for, oh, a hundred years. One of the oldest in the country!"

"How long have you been here?" asked Louscha.

"Nearly as long!" Claudia laughed gaily as they all sat down at the card table. The other women smiled but spoke little, engaged in examining their cards. Claudia turned her birdlike eyes to Stephan. "Bates!"

"Oh — yes," said Stephan, looking down at his shirt. "I went there, once." He'd worn it in hopes of lending his mother some credibility, showing that her son went to a good college. In truth, the education seemed wasted; it had just added loan debt to his stubbornly mediocre life. But they didn't have to know that — although, given that this was the only retirement home he could afford, they would probably guess.

"How wonderful," continued Claudia. "My daughter went to Colby. She's dead now, I'm afraid." She spoke with the practiced air of one who's processed a tragedy to the point of imitation.

"I'm so sorry," said Louscha. "How terrible, to outlive your child."

"Oh, I don't like to hear that," snapped Claudia. "This weighting of lives based on their generations. As though you dwindle in value as you age! But you don't have to dwindle. Why shouldn't we be worth *more*, after all this time?"

Louscha smiled timidly, not without a guilty look at Stephan. "I've always felt the same! We've invested so much in our lives! Why, it's only now — retired, and with Stephan grown — that I feel I can truly focus on myself."

Stephan, left out, tried to focus on looking pleasant. The other women at the table cast sneaky glances at him as they shuffled cards and murmured. They looked good, he had to admit. Healthy and happy. Not like the others, wasted away.

He realized with a start that one of the wasted was right next to him, as though suddenly materialized. He must have missed her when he sat down; now her bowed silver head was directly at his elbow. She was hunched over the table so he couldn't see her face, only her limp gray ponytail and bony shoulders. She didn't seem to fit in at the table, but the other women ignored her.

"In every other field," Claudia was saying, "art, wine, architecture — value increases with age. Why do only humans —" she tapped her chest "—go the opposite way?"

The old woman's head nodded and fell onto Stephan's forearm. He could feel warm breath on his arm hairs — and then a horrible wetness, as though she might be drooling. He tried gingerly to pull his arm away, but she was dead weight; he would send her thunking to the table. He didn't want to make a scene, to embarrass his mother in front of her new friends.

"You know there are two types of people," Claudia was saying. "Those who seize the moment, and those who are overcome by it. A bit flowery, I know. But you are at a crossroads, dear. You must ask yourself, did you come here to die? Or did you come to live? Both decisions are in this room." She waved her hand: at her friends, hale and active, and then at the shoals of shuffling elders. "You have not answered all the questions of your life, dear. There is one more."

Louscha was gazing at Claudia, enraptured, but Stephan could think only of the old woman asleep on his arm. He was sure he felt her lips, even her tongue, even… .

He shrieked abruptly and leaped up. The old crone's head hit the table with a loud crack. She didn't move; she lay like dead weight, face down, one arm dangling.

Her mouth had opened. No teeth, only gums…gnawing at him. Mouthing him. Her tongue licking. Like she was sucking at him, like she wanted to give him a hickey. He cringed, rubbing his arm and smearing her saliva into it.

The gymnasium was silent. The women at the table stared inscrutably. The wraiths ignored them. The woman was face down, only her hair visible. He'd still never seen her features.

And his mother — his mother had ended up on the floor. Had Stephan bumped her as he leapt up? She was prostrate, looking up at him — accusingly? Disheveled in a way that seemed humiliating.

He crouched to help her up. "I'm sorry," he said. "She — she drooled on me or something. It was just gross, is all."

Claudia stood briskly, taking charge. "Let's get you to your room," she said, ignoring the old crone. "You'll want to settle in before dinner, and perhaps a little rest." When he looked back, on his way out, the woman still hadn't moved. No orderly appeared to help.

They walked together through a maze of hallways studded with doors. "The back way to the rooms," Claudia explained. Each door had a little peephole, often surrounded by pictures summarizing the inhabitant's life: diplomas, pictures of Egypt.

Stephan hung behind, examining the art, still embarrassed. A print depicting a family in a carriage, racing through a forest at night. Behind them ran a pack of wolves. The anguished mother held a baby aloft, ready to throw.

Louscha and Claudia were deep in conversation. Whatever they were talking about, it seemed emotional. Louscha kept looking back at Stephan, as though making sure he was still there. Claudia did most of the talking.

She left them at Louscha's door, with a cheery WELCOME! banner taped to it. "My daughter would have liked you," she said to Stephan. "Bates!" She gave him a sudden hug. "Children…such a solace to their elders. Such a balm."

"Remember," she said to Louscha as she left. "One more decision left to make. I hope I see you for breakfast."

"She's certainly intense," Stephan said, once they were alone in her small room. "A little creepy."

"She's right, though," said Louscha. She was puttering around, facing away. "I'd seen this move as — well, as sort of the end. I imagined that I would come here and just…wait. She's shown me that there's more to it than that."

The stark honesty brought his guilt rushing back. "I could sell my condo," he blurted. "We could buy you into a better place, if you don't want to live with me."

Louscha still had her back turned, but she stiffened. Once again, they both knew he didn't really want to. "Oh no," she said. "I couldn't ask you to do something like that." She turned, and suddenly she looked ancient to Stephan: stooped and careworn, her mouth turned down. She'd gotten so old. She was so frail. "No,

I will do quite nicely just where I am. Just…would you stay here tonight?"

Stephan started. In this place of — but he tried to control his expression. What kind of son would he be, if he refused to stay one night where his mother would spend the rest of hers? "Of course," he said. "I'll sleep on the couch."

"Thank you, dear." She smiled; but there was sadness behind it, he thought, hidden in the lines of her face. "Maybe a last night together. Just the two of us, like when we were younger."

She changed into a heavy nightgown in the tiny bathroom, and they settled on the couch to watch TV.

"Do you remember where the vending machine is?" she asked, after a while.

"Not really."

"It's just back towards the common room. Why don't you get us some treats? A candy bar!" She pushed some money towards him.

"I don't know," he said. It had been a terrible day, and a guilty part of him felt that the sooner he went to sleep, the sooner it would be over. The sooner it would be morning, and he could leave.

"Remember the time I picked you up early from school and we went to get ice cream?" she said. He did remember. It was in first grade. The spontaneity, the wild love of it, the knowledge that she'd chosen him above grown-up things, had electrified him. For the rest of elementary school, at that exact time, he looked for her. She'd never done it again.

In some way, though, she'd played a card that made it impossible for him to refuse. He took the money and padded barefoot into the silent hallway. He wandered away, trying to navigate by the pictures on the doors. Egypt. Diploma. A watercolor landscape.

The carpet was intricately patterned, probably to cover stains. Accidents, of one kind or another. But in the dim light it made the floor a miasma, so he didn't see the sharp thing he stepped on. Hissing with pain and hopping on one foot, he brought the other up to examine the wound.

It was a tooth. A human canine, he guessed, stuck right into the sole by its sharp-fanged roots. He gave a whimper of disgust and yanked at it. It was stuck fast and hard to remove. In the dim light, the roots seemed to grasp hungrily as he flung it away, like they were alive.

The tooth had gone surprisingly deep. His foot was bleeding; he hoped the carpet pattern would cover the stains.

Ahead was a stuttering shadow, and the dim light played tricks on his eyes: it looked like a shadow with no body, or the carpet itself creeping up the walls. But no: it was a frail old woman, shuffling along at an infinitely slow rate.

It was the same old crone who'd gummed him in the common room.

Surely too coincidental, though; many old women looked the same from the back. He'd never seen her face, or this woman's either. Just the lank gray ponytail. Her head, too, was bowed down.

There seemed to be no staff around at all. He hadn't seen anyone since they sedated the senile woman. And did this woman need help? Was she even supposed to be out? She tottered resolutely forward, inching her walker and shuffling to meet it. He considered tiptoeing away, not getting involved, returning to his mother's room to say he couldn't find the vending machine.

It was only the two of them here, though. He couldn't leave her. She might be alone, with no one to care for her. He imagined his mother, perhaps, someday, shuffling down this same hall alone. Someone else's son walking away.

He limped up next to the crone. She continued to inch along the wall, giving no indication that she knew he was there. He was sure, now, that it was the woman from the gymnasium.

"Hey," he said. "Do you need help?"

At his voice, she stopped short. She only came up to his sternum, hunched as she was over her walker. Her hands, pale parchment over bulbous veins. She wore a shabby, baggy housedress, with a thin blue bathrobe over it. She halted, but she didn't turn her head or make a sound.

There was a series of small plopping noises on the carpet under her.

"Oh," he said, revulsed and uncertain. She seemed frozen in place. God, had she had an accident? Was it his fault? The sound was like…he pictured rabbit poops falling out from her housedress. He stepped back, looking gingerly down.

Little white things glimmered on the carpet.

He knelt.

They were teeth. A handful of teeth scattered under the hem of her dress. As he looked, a few more pattered down.

A sharp pain in his knee, although he'd looked before he knelt. But it was a tooth, embedded. He whimpered with a disgust verging on panic and yanked it out. It was like a tick, the way it clutched the flesh and had to be torn free. Its roots like little legs, waving indignantly. He looked up to see, for the first time, the crone's face.

It was all holes.

A mouth like a cavern, lipless, wet. No eyes at all. Black hole sockets. Tunnels.

She worked her mouth. It seemed like she might speak; but then she convulsed, like a cat hocking up a hairball, grimacing, and Stephan had no time to move before she opened her dark mouth wide and vomited on him.

It caught him on his left side mostly, on his arm and leg. A blackish clear liquid, viscous; and inside were jagged white pellets. Teeth, and more teeth, and he barely had time to register revulsion before he registered pain. Where they landed they stuck. Where they splashed on him they bit. They embedded. They dug in.

Stephan made a choking noise, sprawling away from the old woman, scraping at his body. There was one in his cheek, wiggling deeper. Quickly through the flesh, probing at muscle. He tore at it wildly. His arm was dotted with teeth, each squirming in like a beetle scrabbling into earth when exposed by a lifted rock. It hurt in a writhing, alien way. He plucked some out and flung them away; but others sank deeper by the moment.

The old woman shuffled painstakingly towards him, her caverned face fixed on his.

He dug his heels into the carpet, pushing away. Still trying to pick the teeth out. His shirt had pulled up, and they'd attached in the fish-white gap above his waistband. Busy, worming. They went root-first, and already some were flush against flesh, icebergs inside him, limned in blood.

The crone inched forward, throat bobbing as though she would vomit again. Stephan whined with terror, limped to his feet and dragged himself down the hall. His left leg didn't work well anymore.

The teeth disappeared as he fled, leaving potholes of blood. He whined and dug his fingers after them, but it hurt too much; he felt their hard enamel inside him, but he couldn't grasp it.

He slumped into a door; but when he turned to knock, an eye was already there. Magnified owlish in the peephole.

He knocked anyway. "Please, can you let me in? I need to come in. I need help."

The eye blinked but didn't move away. There was no sound from behind the door.

The old woman was only a few feet away. He stumbled off, dragging his leg. The teeth inside him carved tunnels like an ant farm.

An eye watched from every peephole, but no door opened.

"It hurts so bad!" he cried. "Please, you're supposed to help! You're supposed to help!"

"She's made her choice," said a soft voice from behind a door. "I'm sorry, young man. It always has to be someone."

"Not me!" he said, throwing himself against the door. "I don't even live here!"

But there was no further answer, and when he looked back the old woman was close enough to grasp at him: her face once again bowed and hidden, skinny arm outstretched. Stephan staggered backwards and ran away, lost in the corridor maze, looking for his mother.

Wolves, diploma. Egypt. And there it was: the bright "WEL-COME!" sign.

A wave of relief. A mother's door will always open.

"Mom!" he sobbed, slumping against the door and turning the handle.

It was locked.

"Mom?" he called through the door. "Mom, can you unlock the door? It's me, I'm just outside."

He thought he heard movement, but the handle was frozen.

He banged on the door, scratched at it, tearing the WELCOME! sign to uncover the keyhole.

His mother's eye was owled behind it.

The crone turned the corner, head still bowed. Clunk-clunk, shuffle. Clunk-clunk, shuffle.

"Mom, the door's locked," he said. "I'm hurt. I got hurt."
Inside him, things popped and spilled.

"I'm so sorry," came his mother's voice, finally. "But I've
learned so much already. Claudia's right, Stephy. There are those
who sacrifice everything, and those who are sacrificed."

"But it's supposed to be you, Mommy," he cried. He sank to the
floor, weakened, bleeding from all his small holes, reaching up
towards the peephole. The walker clunked nearer, nearer. "It's
supposed to be you. That's the point of mothers."

"Oh, my darling," said Louscha through the door. "No it isn't."

The crone loomed over with her face of caves. She bent down,
wet lips writhing, eager for him. Beginning, once again, to retch.

~

CLAUDIA CAME to Louscha's room in the morning to bring her to breakfast. "There you are!" she cried, beaming when Louscha opened the door. "You look wonderful, dear."

The hallway was bright and calm; there was no sign of a disturbance. They wove their way through the ancient walkers tottering through the halls. Claudia pushed roughly by one, who swayed into the wall with a soft whimper. A faded old Bates t-shirt hung baggy on his sunken frame. His eyes were pale and vacant.

Louscha looked back, squinting, and drew breath as though to speak, but Claudia caught her arm and dragged her on. "Don't worry," she said. "He probably didn't even notice. Breakfast shuts down in an hour and I have so much to tell you. You'll be so happy here. And you deserve to be happy, dear. After all, as a mother, how much have you sacrificed?"

Louscha turned away, nodding in fervent agreement. "Oh, everything!" she exclaimed. "Everything!"

The Macabre Reader

Lysette Stevenson

EERIE PUBLICATIONS THE COMPLETE COVERS: The Whole Bloody Mess BY MIKE HOWLETT. *Fantaco Enterprises, 2022.* Cover art by Bill Alexander, 1970.

In early 1950's America, the Comic Code Authority was enacted out of public concern that images of graphic violence, nudity and horror were encouraging moral delinquency in youth. While the pressure was put on the comic industry, horror publishers such as Warren and Skywald, used a work around by switching to magazines. Publisher and comic artist, Myron Fass, jumped on the trend to make a quick buck.

Myron's magazine contents were not original, instead they were black and white reprints of pre and post code horror. What he capitalized on was standing out from the competition, with covers that were eye-catchingly garish and gore laden, in essence, everything the CCA was trying to suppress. His main objective was winning the consumer's dollar first and in some instances sent the art to print before it was even completed. He would collage work from other covers or boldly pirated from publications like the German space opera series: *Perry Rhodan*. It was the wild west of horror illustration but despite his dubious practices, he employed many talented and respected artists to create covers unlike anything else on the newsstands.

Mike Howlett uses his personal collection to produce this lowbrow, high quality coffee table book. The covers are full size and in vivid color so you can examine every illustrated minutia of a truly weird and wonderful period of pulp horror excess.

~

MANX TALES of Horror BY A J LERT. *Gordon Publishers, 1974.*

In this slim, hundred-page chapbook we are introduced to classic tropes of horror, all notably set within the Isle of Man. Despite their close proximity to England and Ireland, the Manx are very much their own people with a mixture of Celtic and Viking heritage. A craggy island perched in the northern Irish sea, to most, the Isle stirs up images of seafaring folk and a bucolic windswept countryside. According to A J Lert, beyond the veil of this civilization is a witch haunted isle filled with ghosts, demons, and hobgoblins. Through the shrouds of sea mist lurks spectral black dogs and churchyard spirits.

It is an endearing collection of hyper-local weird tales. A phantom uses violence to protect its grand old opera house from redevelopment; a London sexual sadist takes a holiday to the Isle and tries to pick up a local vampire. In each of the stories there's a strong sense of camp and black humor. A group of salesmen spending the weekend in an eerie manor house make a fool's errand by mocking its legendary status. In a tale of high drama, a wiccan priest calls a great sabbat in the countryside to counter a satanic cabal. It wouldn't be the Isle of Man if it didn't have a story involving the iconic TT motorcycle race and a psychic premonition. This collection is ominously eccentric and distinctly Manx.

~

THE LAZARUS INHERITANCE BY NOEL VREELAND CARTER. *Popular Library Gothic, 1976.*

Gillian Lazarus spent her childhood locked away in a tower. Told that she carried her father's bloodline curse, a form of vampirism that drained the life force from anyone she touched. One night her father allegedly murders her mother and comes for Gillian. Her governess rescues her, after locking her father in the tower and they run off into the woods.

The story begins nine years later, with Gillian burying her governess and setting off to claim her birthright. Despite the warnings to stay away, she returns to New England where her memories arc an unreliable mixture of fantasy and terror. When she arrives at her family home, she meets her cousin, curiously a spitting image of her father, who had assumed accession of the property. The narrative shifts between their blossoming relationship and the familial comfort of her aunt and her border, a kindly priest and his bullmastiff. As Gillian tries to piece together the events of her childhood, her mental and physical state collapses. She has vivid recurring nightmares where she is trapped inside the skeletal ribcage of her father, encased in a jeweled spider web.

Carter eschews the trope of a helpless maiden in peril and brings to life a moody, self determined, proto-goth; torn between two worlds and the legacy of her inheritance. Noel Vreeland Carter, only wrote a small handful of Gothics, which are becoming increasingly hard to find. Frustratingly so, as I would like to read them all. She was the wife of fantasy author, editor and raconteur, Lin Carter.

~

THROUGH THE NIGHT LIKE A SNAKE: Latin American Horror Stories. *Two Lines Press, 2024.*

Ten short stories ranging from the weird to the horrific with writers in translation from across Latin America. An exciting and distinctive anthology, it is a great introduction to newly translated authors while featuring writers already popular in translation like Maria Enriquez, Monica Ojeda and Claudia Hernandez.

Throughout this collection there's an undercurrent of corrupt politics, fascism and dictatorships. Some speak directly to the struggle for survival, such as when a starving, nomadic family shelters in an abandoned house with open graves in the yard. While others engage with the menace of the wilderness, like when a young woman terrified of the mountains takes a solo trip to see her dying grandfather. Societal issues are explored when a satanic nunnery cloisters an exploited trans woman, or the absurd posturing of neighbors attempting to be civil with a vulture man after he has eaten their dog and is hungrily eyeing up their children. Each of these unique and surreal stories excavate from a wealth of human cruelty and darkness.

Launched in early 2020, the Calico Series is an imprint of San Francisco based Two Lines Press, featuring translated work within the vanguard of literature and poetry. *Through the Night Like a Snake* is their ninth installment. Other collections have featured Chinese speculative fiction, Russian, Haitian and Arabic poetry, Swahili Afrofuturism and a forthcoming collection of Romanian poetry.

~

MORTAL HUNGER: A Novel Based on the Life of Lafcadio Hearn BY HARRY WEDECK. *Sheridan House, 1947.*

Lafcadio Hearn deliberately sought out the macabre and fantastic, so much so, you almost can't believe that this is based on the true accounts of his incredible life. Born in Greece in 1850, and raised in Ireland, he was abandoned by his family members, shuffled from guardianship to boarding school. He excelled in writing and translating, most notably from French to English: Maupassant, Gautier and Flaubert. At the age of nineteen, he emigrated to the United States with five dollars in his pocket and found success as a journalist reporting on true crime and weird phenomena in Cincinnati. He moved to New Orleans, writing extensively on Creole culture and Louisiana voodoo. After a short stay in the West Indies, an opportunity arose to teach in Japan. It was there that he wrote what he is most known for, *Kwaidan: Stories and Studies of Strange Things*, a collection of Japanese folklore translated into English. While it introduced the western world to the ghost tales of the east, it simultaneously captured a Japan that was rapidly disappearing with the age of industrialization.

Despite being Harry Wedeck's only novel, he does an excellent job bringing the vibrancy, high jinks and passion of Lafcadio's adventures into an engaging narrative. Harry Wedeck went on to write popular books on magic, the occult and witchcraft for New York's Philosophical Library.

TWISTED CLAY BY FRANK WALFORD. *Remains Books, 2014.* First published, 1933.

Twisted Clay is a raucous Australian thriller, set in the blue mountain range of New South Wales. Jean Desaline is born during a wicked storm. At a young age she discovers her power as a femme fatale. Seducing her maid, tormenting her grandmother and using her beauty to manipulate men and women to her will. At the time in Australia, homosexuality was considered a form of mental illness. This caused Jean to feel like an aberration. She tries to take her own life by boiling herself to death in the laundry tub. When her suicide attempt fails, she resolves to embrace her true self.

After Jean overhears her father and doctor's intention to send her to conversion therapy in Europe, she devises a plan to save herself at all costs. She murders her beloved father and plots against the doctor. Her dead father begins to haunt her, begging her to dig him up and bandage the hole in his head, and that's just getting started.

Written as Jean's journal, you get a front seat narration to the most delightfully unhinged protagonist. Young, beautiful, precocious and fighting for her life. You couldn't help but root for her even though she's on a murderous spree. Banned shortly after its release and therefore expensive to track down, Remains Books keeps it affordably in print for all to enjoy.

〜

MIDNIGHT STORM MOONLESS SKY: Indigenous Horror Stories BY ALEX SOOP. *Durville & UpRoute Books, 2022.* Interior illustrations by Alex and Patricia Soop.

Alex grew up on the Blood Reserve in Southern Alberta, where in 2018, he spent five years incarcerated in the Drumheller penitentiary. Soop said writing became a way of coping, keeping his head down to avoid the destructive cycle of addiction and violence in prison. After his time was served and while attending community college, his talent for storytelling was recognised and encouraged.

This is the first of two collections published through Durville Books. *Midnight Storms Moonless Sky* is a riveting and personal account of contemporary indigenous life with elements of the supernatural woven in. Using lore and legends like an origin story for the wendigo, as well as a morbid fascination with the abandoned residential school near his home, Soop works through the darkness that had transpired in his life. Nowhere is safe in Alex's world, as werewolves roam the countryside, he incorporates real locations in his stories such as when a traveler hitchhikes the Highway of Tears, a notorious stretch of road where indigenous women have gone missing from. His lived experiences inhabit the characters even as they encounter the fantastic, like when promises are hard kept by prison inmates to dispose of a possessed dagger. His voice and candor glide smoothly through each of these dark tales. While the objective of the stories are to entertain, they also let the reader in on the real-life horrors indigenous people continue to grapple with today.

~

LUCIFER and the Child BY ETHEL MANNIN. *Swan River Press, 2020.* First published, 1945. Dust jacket art, Lorena Carrington.

It was initially banned on its release for its depiction of a willful and resourceful young girl embracing witchcraft, defying her godparents and slipping away to spend her hours in the slums with a reviled old crone. Here we are introduced to Jenny Flower, born on Hallowe'en, to a lineage of relatives burned in the 1600's during the witch trials. Her mother Nell, an escort and a bartender, turns the child over to her religious brother and sister-in-law to raise. One fateful afternoon she meets a horned man in the woods who charmingly greets her with "Hullo witch!" She dedicates her life to him and wishes they would be together forever, as he magically appears on her birthdays and special sabbaths. It is up for interpretation if he really is the King of the Witches, or a sailor and former lover of her mother. Ethel blends in just enough magic to keep you suspended between both worlds and swept up in Jenny's fantasy. The young girl is so passionate for her freedom, you believe in her even as she delves into paths darker than her experience can master.

Ethel Mannin is known for her journalism, prolific memoirs and her activism in socialist and anti-fascist movements. She moved in circles with W.B Yeats, Bertrand Russell, Emma Goldman and had an iconic portrait photographed by Paul Tanqueray. It was almost forgotten that she had written a supernatural tale set in 1940's London on the heels of the second world war. Picking up where Machen left off with *The White People, Lucifer and the Child* is a rich and vibrant feminist take on the occult arts and prewar peril.

Contributors

Seán Padraic Birnie is a writer from Brighton. His fiction has appeared in venues such as *Best British Short Stories 2022*, *The Year's Best Dark Fantasy & Horror Vol. 3*, *The Dark*, *Interzone*, and *ergot*. In 2021 Undertow Publications published his debut collection of short stories, *I Would Haunt You if I Could*. He is on Bluesky and Instagram @seanbirnie. For more information, see seanbirnie.com

Derrick Boden's fiction has appeared in *Lightspeed*, *Clarkesworld*, *Apex Magazine*, and elsewhere. Derrick is a Sturgeon Award-nominated writer, a software developer, an adventurer, and a graduate of the Clarion West class of 2019. He currently calls Boston his home, although he's lived in fourteen cities spanning four continents. He is owned by two cats and one iron-willed daughter. Find him at derrickboden.com and on Twitter as @derrickboden.

Gordon Brown grew up in the deserts of Syria and now lives in the deserts of Nevada. Since arriving in the New World, his work has appeared in *McSweeney's Internet Tendency*, *Hunger Mountain Review*, *Tales to Terrify*, *Chthonic Matter Quarterly*, and elsewhere. He spends his time writing feverishly and looking after his cats, of which he has none.

Sasha Brown is a Boston writer, gardener and dad whose surreal stories have been called "Creative! But in a bad way." He's in lit mags like *X-Ray* and *Masters Review*, and in genre pubs like *Bourbon Penn* and *F&SF*. He's on twitter @dantonsix and online at sashabrownwriter.com.

Hiron Ennes is the British Fantasy Award-winning author of *Leech*. In their spare time, they're a rogue harpist and a mad doctor. Their areas of interest include forensics, infectious disease, and petting your dog.

Corey Farrenkopf lives on Cape Cod with his wife, Gabrielle, and works as a librarian. His work has been published in/is forthcoming from *Nightmare, Electric Literature, The Deadlands, Vastarien, The Southwest Review, Bourbon Penn, SmokeLong Quarterly*, and elsewhere. His debut novel, *Living in Cemeteries*, was released from JournalStone in April of 2024. He is the Fiction Editor for *The Cape Cod Poetry Review*. To learn more, follow him on twitter @CoreyFarrenkopf or on the web at CoreyFarrenkopf.com

Jason Fernandes is an attorney and speculative fiction writer in Washington, D.C. He is a graduate of the Odyssey Writing Workshop and the recipient of the 2024 Kurt Vonnegut Speculative Fiction Prize. His fiction has recently appeared in *North American Review* and *Hemingway Shorts*.

Orrin Grey is a skeleton who likes monsters as well as the author of several spooky books. His stories of ghosts, monsters, and sometimes the ghosts of monsters can be found in dozens of anthologies, including Ellen Datlow's *Best Horror of the Year*. He resides in the suburbs of Kansas City and watches lots of scary movies. You can visit him online at orringrey.com

Vince Haig is an illustrator, designer, and author. You can visit Vince at his website: barquing.com

Avra Margariti is a queer author, Greek sea monster, and Rhysling-nominated poet with a fondness for the dark and the darling. Avra's work haunts publications such as *Strange Horizons*,

The Deadlands, Three-Lobed Burning Eye, F&SF, Asimov's, and *Vastarien.* You can find Avra on twitter (@avramargariti).

David Nickle is an award-winning author of numerous short stories and novels. His most recent novel is *Volk: A Novel of Radiant Abomination,* concluding the "Book of the Juke" series begun with *Eutopia: A Novel of Terrible Optimism.* Some of his stories are collected in *Monstrous Affections,* and *Knife Fight and Other Struggles.* His home online is at davidnickle.ca

Mike O'Driscoll's fiction has appeared in *Black Static, The Magazine of Fantasy and Science Fiction, Interzone, Crime Wave* and anthologies including *Best New Horror,* and *Year's Best Fantasy & Horror.* Two collections of stories, *Unbecoming* and *The Dream Operator,* were published by Elastic Press and Undertow, and his story, *Eyepennies,* appeared as the first of TTA Press's series of stand alone novellas, in 2012. His story, *Sounds Like,* was adapted by Brad Anderson for an episode of the horror anthology show, *Masters of Horror.*

Jorja Osha is a speculative fiction writer living on the East Coast. When not writing about otherworldly beings, troubled characters and everything else in between she can usually be found playing video games, listening to music or building things. Her work has previously appeared in or are forthcoming in *The Dark, Apparition Lit,* and *Beyond the Bounds of Infinity,* an anthology published by Raw Dog Screaming Press. She used to write under the pen name Bibi Osha appearing in *NIGHTLIGHT, The Dark, A Coup of Owls* and *Martian.*

Nelson Stanley lives and works in Bristol, U.K. He's had short fiction published in places such as *The Dark, Old Moon Quarterly, Vastarien,* and *Kaleidotrope.*

Lysette Stevenson is a stage manager with a rural outdoor equestrian theatre company and a second generation bookseller. She lives in British Columbia.

Simon Strantzas is the author of five collections of short fiction, including *Only the Living Are Lost* (Hippocampus Press, 2023), and editor of a number of anthologies, including *Year's Best Weird Fiction, Vol. 3*. Combined, he's been a finalist for four Shirley Jackson Awards, two British Fantasy Awards, and the World Fantasy Award. His fiction has appeared in numerous annual best-of anthologies, and in venues such as *Nightmare*, *The Dark*, and *Cemetery Dance*. In 2014, his edited anthology, *Aickman's Heirs*, won the Shirley Jackson Award. He lives with his wife in Toronto, Canada.

www.ingramcontent.com/pod-product-compliance
Lightning Source LLC
Chambersburg PA
CBHW020344260626
47156CB00004B/1679